*AQUA FOLLIES*
LivRancourt.com

Copyright © 2017 by Amy Dunn Caldwell
Cover Art: Kanaxa
Developmental Editor: KJ Charles
Editor: Linda Ingmanson
Proofreader: Michael Valsted

ISBN-10: 0-9985822-3-9
ISBN-13: 978-0-9985822-3-8

This is a work of fiction. Names, characters, places, businesses and incidents either are the product of the author's imagination or are used fictitiously. Any resemblance to actual persons, living or dead, events, or locales is entirely coincidental.

Interior Format

# Aqua Follies

# Follies

## LIV RANCOURT

# The 1950s.

## POSTWAR EXUBERANCE. CONFORMITY. ROCK AND ROLL.

## HOMOPHOBIA.

RUSSELL TELLS HIMSELF HE'LL MARRY Susie because it's the right thing to do. His summer job coaching her water ballet team will give him plenty of opportunity to give her a ring. But on the team's trip to the annual Aqua Follies, the joyful glide of a trumpet player's solo hits Russell like a torpedo, blowing apart his carefully constructed plans.

From the orchestra pit, Skip watches Poseidon's younger brother stalk along the pool deck. It never hurts to smile at a man, because good things might happen. Once the last note has been played, Skip gives it a shot.

The tenuous connection forged by a simple smile leads to events that dismantle both their lives. Has the damage been done, or can they pick up the pieces together?

*This book is dedicated to all the men who should now be leaders in the arts, in science, in business, and in every other profession, but who did not survive the 1980s.*
*You are often in my thoughts.*

# Chapter 1

❦

*A*QUA FOLLIES OF 1955 read the handbills plastered to every smooth surface. *OLYMPIC CHAMPIONS. STAGE & POOL STARS.*
   *CELEBRATE SEAFAIR!*

Russell rubbed his hands together, trying to warm up, trying to find the silver lining under the sodden gray sky.

Trying to remember why he let his aunt talk him into taking this job anyway.

The twenty-four Aqua Dears paddled in place, their white swim caps bobbing like a line of water lilies in the indigo water. The swimmers were better off, since the lake water was warmer than the chilly damp air. *Damn.* Seattle in July was colder than Minneapolis in April or even March. Russell glared at the overcast, washed-out sunset. Of course, if he'd stayed home in Red Wing, he'd still be withering under the chill of his parents' melancholy.

Reason enough to come west.

Bleachers fanned out tall and white along the edge of the lake. Russell grabbed a seat on one end and pulled a small, spiral-bound notebook from his pocket. In the last routine, Phyllis had drifted too far to the left during the cadence action, dragging half the line with her. He made a note to talk to her, then sketched the pool, a segment of the lake separated by the half-moon curve of the stage. His best guess put the stage at forty feet long, and given the layout, the girls would need to watch for the diving towers on either end to stay oriented.

The girls' Aqua Tropicana number began with deck work. He was sketching a diagram of the pool side, marking their positions, when someone called his name.

"Ssst, Russ."

The whisper came from the far end of the line, the end with the short girls. Susie Bradford was the shortest, and the most likely to complain. She had many good qualities. Patience didn't make the list.

He kept his eyes on his notebook because he didn't want to encourage her. She'd get them both in trouble, and as the team's coach, Aunt Maude would have another reason to be disappointed in him. As the assistant coach, he tried to lead by example. As his girlfriend, Susie tried to take advantage of his position.

Across the pool, the show's director cornered Aunt Maude. She stood like a bulwark of decorum in the face of an impressive amount of arm waving. Figuring the guy might be more likely to stand aside if she had a man behind her, Russell rose and strolled across the deck in her general direction.

She didn't need his help. Her swimmers had been in the water for almost two hours, and she would get them finished on time, no matter how showy the director's tantrum.

Keeping his head high and shoulders broad, Russell retraced his steps. His pride was salvaged some when Susie hissed at him again. She sculled down low in the water, a steady line of bubbles popping to the surface from the direction of her mouth. He shrugged and held his hands out, palms up. She raised her chin out of the water. *Cold*, she mouthed.

He glanced over at his aunt, then back at Susie. "Sorry." All the girls had to be pretty soggy.

"I got first dibs on the shower," Susie said, raising her voice high enough for the others to hear.

"Race you," someone whispered back.

"You're on." Susie flicked water in the direction of the voice.

Russell made a fierce karate chop with his hand, trying to quiet her, but the other swimmer egged her on. "My legs are longer."

"But I'm sneakier." Susie giggled loud enough to earn a hard stare from his aunt. She lowered herself in the water, and Russell reached for his whistle. He could always keep the girls occupied with practicing some basic figures to get a feel for the pool.

Aunt Maude patted the director's shoulder and strode downstage, mistress of all she saw. "Hop out, girls." She clapped her hands briskly. "Grab towels if you need them. We'll go through the last few numbers and go home."

Right away, Susie scuttled over to Russell. "After all this, I'll need a shot of whiskey to take the chill off."

"Me too." Russell smirked to temper the truth in his words. "Go get your robe."

"Nah, you'll keep me warm enough."

He took pity on her shivering and draped an arm over her shoulders. She tucked herself in close, ensuring he'd be left with soggy spots on his sports shirt and khaki slacks, but he didn't push her away.

He and Susie made a good team, and for the seven thousandth time, he wished the press of her curves put more heat in his veins.

No such luck.

"Thanks, lamb chop." Her rubber nose clip gave her voice a nasal hum, and she trembled in the cool summer air. "Can we sneak out later?"

"Sure, but if Aunt Maude catches us, we'll both be on the train back home."

She faked kicking him in the shin. "I didn't come all this way to worry about going home. You and me are going to have fun."

He pressed a kiss on the top of her head. "Yes, dear."

Their last hurrah. They had two weeks in Seattle, then another run in Detroit. At some point, Russell would give Susie the diamond ring he had tucked in the bottom of his suitcase. He snugged her closer to his side. He'd start his new job, they'd get hitched, he'd buy the house, and she'd give him babies. More importantly, the wedding would give his parents something to be happy about.

The feeling of dread wedged under his sternum had more to do with nerves than anything else.

The director called for the Night at Club Aqua

number and counted off a fast tempo. His baton
flashed in the floodlights blazing from the edge of
the stage. From the orchestra pit, the band hit the
opening bars of "In the Mood." Susie took off, diving into action with the other Aqua Dears. They
spun through the water in a synchronized display,
while the dancing half of their traveling troupe, the
Aqua Darlings, took the stage dressed in sparkling
blue skirts, white blouses, and low-heeled black
shoes.

The big band, a dozen musicians playing brass
and strings and percussion, romped through the
verses twice, their heads silhouetted in the stage
lights. Then a lone musician stood, rising into the
glare like Gary Cooper on the screen at a drive-in
movie. He was tall and lean and handsome, with
a curled pompadour and a five-o'clock shadow.
Curiosity pinned Russell in place. Then the young
man put a trumpet to his lips, and Russell had to
close his eyes.

The music rang out over the lake and bounced
off the rooftops in the surrounding neighborhood.
The tone was cool, but the solo was hot, hitting
Russell with the force of a pickax. The horn's
voice turned his insides to jelly, but the man—from
the swoop of his hair to the curve of his bicep—
swapped that jelly for lava.

He tried to tell himself his damp clothes caused
the shivers chasing over his skin, but didn't come
close to believing it. He dug his fingertips into the
bands of muscle running up the back of his own
neck and dragged his gaze back to the swimmers,
breathing slow and deep to force the flush out of

his face. He'd just been surprised by the man, and exhausted from travel. He'd be fine. Everything was okay.

After an age and a half, the Aqua Dears hopped out of the water, clearing the pool for the divers, whose acrobatic shenanigans marked the end of the number. All four of the divers had competed in the Olympics, but for the Aqua Follies, they splashed the crowd with goofy tricks. Everyone knew they were the highlight of the show. The Dears could swim and the Darlings could dance, but the divers in clown suits were what people talked about walking out to their cars.

Russell needed the break, because he didn't quite have a grip on himself when the music ended. Fortunately, Susie stayed with the other swimmers. There were limits to how far he could push his charade.

*It's not a charade.* Fooling around with the trumpet player would be the fantasy. A farce, even. He'd known Susie since they were kids. He liked her smile and he liked her spunk. They were good for each other. Still, he had to bow his head to drive the sound of the horn out of his mind.

Susie and the other Dears took their positions along the edge of the pool, and the show's headliner came out to sing "Papa Loves Mambo." Now wearing floral sarong skirts, the Darlings shimmied onto the stage. Almost all of them made it through the dance with their towering fake fruit headdresses in place.

Russell shook out his slacks, pulling away the damp patch Susie left on his thigh. The Dears dove back into the pool, their sherbet-colored swimsuits making splashes of paint against the iron-gray evening. Russell glanced over at the band, picked out the trumpet player's profile. The swimmers' pale arms moved in perfect rhythm for their crawl-stroke line, wrists cocked and elbows sharp, and when they reached the other side, the group executed a synchronized roll into back layouts. Each girl raised one leg in a ballet kick, their pointed toes making graceful sweeps through the air.

Russell pulled out his spiral notebook, his nubbin of a pencil ready. A hot horn lick drew his eyes away from the pool. His aunt relied on him to monitor the show from the stands, because a lifetime spent on the deck when his older sisters performed in the Aqua Dears taught him what to look for. When his aunt asked, he'd have to be able to describe details from the performance. He wouldn't be able to satisfy her unless he calmed down enough to pay attention. With every ounce of his will, he shut out the music and watched the girls swim.

The rehearsal lasted almost longer than he could stand. Afterwards, he stood with his back to a low brick building separating the amphitheater from the parking lot. He let the soft *shurr* of waves on the stony shore settle his nerves and waited for Susie to come out of the locker room.

His aunt found him there. "Your girlfriend needs to pay more attention."

"She did fine, Aunt Maude." Maude Ogilvie knew more about synchronized swimming than just about anyone else in Minneapolis, but she had a blind spot a mile wide when it came to Susie. If she had her way, she'd cut his friend from the team in a minute, but a committee made the selections, and Susie's talent and charisma secured her spot.

"Fine?" Her curled topknot and flowered housedress were at odds with the toughness in her expression. "She barely made her last entrance."

"Constance struggled a bit with the split rocket combination," he said, giving his aunt something else to chew on. He'd learned the hard way not to pick fights.

"I saw that one too."

"And Phyllis mistimed her dives more than once." A few guys shambled along the path. One carried a guitar case, the other a bulky box probably holding a saxophone. *Not looking for him*. Russell locked his attention on his aunt.

She scratched a note on her pad. "You're right. I'll sit the girls down and talk with them all tonight."

*Shoot*. "What about in the morning? This has been a long day already." The day had started with their train's arrival in Seattle after a thirty-hour trip, so he had no problem sounding sincere.

His aunt squinted at him as if she hoped to find something suspicious. "I'll consider it." She gave the bus a sharp nod. "Coming?"

"I'll be there in a minute."

Several Dears came out of the locker room, their wet hair pulled back in ponytails or covered with bandanas. Most of the girls would wait till they got back to the hotel to set their hair. A few more musicians straggled in from the lake. Still no trumpet player.

Susie bounded out of the locker room, the hems of her dungarees rolled just so, a red cardigan tied by the sleeves around her shoulders, her charm bracelet rattling. Planting herself at Russell's elbow, she let the tilt of her head claim him as her territory. Her grin flashed in the moonlight and her laughter buoyed him, and yes, there it was. The trickle of warmth that let him know he was doing the right thing.

"Is Mom already on the bus?" his cousin Annette asked, her tight pink blouse and Bettie Page bangs emphasizing her status as an Amazonian swimming goddess.

"Yeah, we should go." Russell used his best assistant coach voice, though no one paid any attention.

More girls came out of the locker room and more musicians came up the path from the lake. The two groups meshed together in an escalating commotion. All the musicians wore identical black trousers and white button-down shirts, though some had loosened their ties. Russell would have hollered at the girls, directing them to the bus, but their blushing giggles entertained him. Besides, just then the trumpet player walked up with a short, slight young man whose black eyes reminded Russell of the river otters back home.

Susie nudged her head toward the fun. "Hold on."

The dark-eyed young man approached them, his brash grin aimed right at Susie. Russell's hackles rose, and he pushed through Annette and some of the other girls, ready to show them all he had dibs on the pretty one. So what if a certain trumpet player was watching? Aunt Maude would blow her whistle in about three minutes, and then he'd join the girls on the bus.

For a brief moment, the two groups mingled, the girls' giggles pitching higher and higher. Expression stern, Russell kept a hand on Susie's shoulder, daring the dark-eyed boy to come any closer. Aunt Maude poked her head out of the bus, whistle poised in her mouth. A couple of beats later, she blew it loud enough to startle people in China.

Couldn't make his heart beat any faster, because right before the whistle sounded, the tall, lean trumpet player looked over at Russell, caught his eye, and smiled.

# Chapter 2

## ℭ

THE SHRIEKING BLARE OF THE whistle strafed Russell's ears, and the bottom dropped out of his gut. He flinched away from the sound, fingers flexing on Susie's shoulder.

"Ouch." She elbowed him, bringing him back to himself. The musician's smile had rattled him, but that wasn't the real source of his chagrin.

"Get on the bus," his aunt hollered, waving her arms as if the damned whistle hadn't done enough to get the girls' attention. His face flaming, Russell circled the edge of the group, nudging any stragglers, too shaken to pay attention when Susie bounced toward the back with her friends.

Russell knew how things between men went, but he hadn't been able to help himself. The trumpet player's smile was as bright and sweet and clean as his horn playing. Russell hadn't smiled back, but he hadn't looked away either. He'd held the man's gaze long enough to send a message.

Russell grabbed the seat behind the driver, grateful he didn't have to listen to Susie prattle on until he'd found a measure of calm. He'd distanced himself from his past missteps. The last thing he needed to do was make new ones. Staring down at his clasped hands, he vowed he would keep himself in check. He would do right by his aunt. By his family. By Susie.

He would not take one last look at the trumpet player, over by the women's locker room.

"I need everyone's attention right here." Standing between the two front seats, his aunt interrupted his mental wrestling. She gripped the metal frame of the seat across from him and clutched her clipboard with her other hand. "I want to go over my notes from tonight."

A group groan interrupted her announcement. Russell stretched his legs out under the driver's seat. At least his aunt's lecture would take his mind off the things he couldn't bear to think about. The smile could have meant anything, and despite himself, Russell imagined the possibilities. His heart ticked faster, until he kicked himself for being an idiot.

His aunt focused on her clipboard and ran through her comments on the show, oblivious to the girls' inattention. "And now I want to remind you of a few things," she said. Everyone, even Russell, straightened up.

"We are here as representatives of the city of Minneapolis, and as such, we need to remember how to behave."

Someone snickered, earning a fearsome glare. "As you know, you will perform nightly from now until the thirteenth of August, with two shows on

Friday and Saturday nights. We have arranged activities during the day, and for many of those activities you will be representing the Aqua Dears." She paused as if to let the importance of her statement sink in. "Seafair is a celebration of civic pride, and we must not, in any way, cause a distraction."

Russell rubbed a palm over his mouth to hide the smirk. His aunt's tone of voice didn't give them much to celebrate, and there'd been even less reason in the exhausting train ride and dreary overcast rehearsal.

"You will have three free afternoons."

A muffled snort interrupted her. Maude sent a sharp glance through the late-evening gloom.

"Three free afternoons, and lights out will be at eleven thirty every night."

Many of the girls groaned.

"Any behavior unbecoming a young lady will earn you an early ticket back home, and more importantly, you will lose your spot on the team."

No one had anything smart to say about that. Silence settled over them, disrupted only by the chugging rumble of the bus's engine.

Aunt Maude continued. "Do I need to remind you how a young lady behaves?"

Russell massaged the tightness running across the top of one shoulder. Susie could stand a lesson or two. He figured the odds of them getting in trouble were pretty much fifty-fifty. Without Susie's influence to keep him in check, he'd probably raise those odds to 100%. His aunt beamed out over the girls, all but glowing with propriety, and Russell gave up on the massage. He needed a nice glass of whiskey to stifle her righteousness.

⁌

It was almost midnight when Skip and Ryker slid into the red Naugahyde booth at Beth's Café.

"What's the word from the bird?" Ryker clutched an unlit cigarette between his fingers.

*I saw the man of my dreams.* Skip covered his grin with his hand, picking a tamer response. "I want some red meat."

"You and me both." Ryker lit up, blowing smoke across the table. He was small and dark with a slicked-back duck butt and a greaser's sneer. Whenever the subject came up, he claimed he got his coloring from his little Welsh grandmother. Skip usually asked if the milkman had been Italian.

Ryker usually told Skip to get bent.

Skip recognized most of the usual crowd, the musicians, the waiters, the kind of people who were out and about when late night turned into early morning. He extended his long legs under the table. After so many hours in the aqua theater's small orchestra pit, his knees and calves thanked him for the stretch. Since Ryker was blowing smoke over his half of the table, he guessed he could take up some extra floor space.

The waitress came over, her blue-green uniform barely buttoned over her buxom chest and a fine black net covered her peroxide curls.

"What can I bring you gentlemen?" She directed her question at Skip. He aimed her at Ryker with a good-natured toss of his head, sending curls spilling into his face. All the pomade in the world couldn't make his hair behave.

"How 'bout a burger with a side of titties… um, taters?" Ryker's grin broadened the harder she blushed.

Skip kicked him under the table and gave the waitress an apologetic grin. "I'd like a steak and a large Coke."

She passed them menus and stalked off. Ryker flirted with every woman he came across. He'd meet the right girl at some point, but till then, he put himself at risk for getting slapped unless Skip intervened.

An older, grumpier waitress came to take their order.

"It's your own fault," Skip said, glad there was still a waitress willing to help them. He needed to get to bed before his alarm went off in the morning. Four thirty was gonna come early. Getting to bed after midnight just made him hate his job at Boeing even more.

The grumpy waitress scratched their order on a pad and shuffled off, and Ryker tapped his cigarette against the edge of the plastic ashtray. "I wanna get my hands on that little dark-haired aqua baby we saw tonight."

Skip disguised his laugh by flipping his hair out of his eyes. She was cute, but not his type. None of the water ballet girlies were his type. Their coach, now, the one who'd been stalking along the deck like Poseidon in chinos? Skip didn't try to hide his grin. Tall and broad and clean-cut, he was the kind of man who caught Skip's attention.

A fellow could get arrested if he happened to cross a vice cop, but Skip hadn't been caught yet. He'd give a strange man a friendly smile, just to see what would happen. Tonight he would have had to be dumb and blind not to notice the flash of interest the man at the lake had done his best to hide. Nothing would come of it, but a guy could dream, couldn't he?

The waitress set the plate holding Skip's Spencer steak in front of him, then slammed down Ryker's burger hard enough to make some fries jump off the plate.

"I still think we should go over to Parker's," Ryker said, crushing out his smoke. "The Frantics are doing a show."

Skip applied himself to cutting bites off his steak, the charred-beef scent making his mouth water, the juices pooling cherry red on the white plate. He was a sucker for beef cooked rare, no matter what time of day. "Gotta work in the morning."

"You and your stupid job."

"Just because my daddy doesn't pay my rent…" *Or have anything else to do with me.* Skip planted his elbows on the tabletop and rubbed his palms together. Maybe he didn't know much about his family, but Mom had done her best. He knew it like he knew his own name.

Ryker grimaced over his burger. "All right, but after the show tomorrow, I'm going to grab my little swimming dolly and show her around town."

"Maybe you can take her to watch the submarine races." Skip laughed and ducked the flying french fry. For a rich boy, Ryker was okay. He couldn't keep his mind out of the gutter, but he was usually good for taking care of the check.

And since he lived his life like one of those television soap operas, he didn't question why Skip never had a date.

☙

The night hadn't warmed up any, so Russell changed into blue jeans before he snuck out to the alley. Susie snatched a handful of cookies and two coffee mugs out of the kitchen.

He brought the bottle of whiskey.

They sat side by side on the cool concrete steps outside the back door of Hansee Hall, the dorm where the team was being housed. After pouring a pair of healthy shots, Russell tapped her mug with his own. "Cheers."

She handed him a cookie and tossed back a mouthful of whiskey. "Hoo boy."

"Yes, ma'am." He took a shot and let the whiskey go to work. He didn't want to worry. He didn't want to think. He wanted to listen to Susie's happy chatter and let himself go numb.

"Did you see Phyllis?" Susie swirled the liquid in her mug. "She almost tripped over her tongue when all those boys came up from the lake."

The whiskey's earthy scent was more pleasant than the smell of old garbage and engine oil. "Wasn't watching her," he said, which was true enough. He took a sip, keeping an eye out for university students headed home from a late night in the library. No one needed to know they were out there.

He shifted closer, and Susie settled back against his shoulder. Her petite form stirred gentleman-ly protective urges, the bone-deep certainty he'd put his body between her and anything harmful. Catching a whiff of her powdery floral perfume, he half wanted to take his cock in hand to see if he could raise some other kind of urges.

Though he couldn't treat her so disrespectfully.

Susie sighed and took another swallow. "Your aunt hates me."

"My aunt hates everybody."

The amber porch light washed over Susie's heart-shaped face. Her dark hair had dried in loose curls, and she looked like a green-eyed Elizabeth Taylor. This was it. Time to kiss his girlfriend.

Drumming up courage, Russell poured another splash in her mug. "We'll just stay out of her way."

"Sure." She lolled against him with a half smile. He lowered his head, aiming vaguely for her lips. She giggled and scooted away.

This was their game. He maneuvered, she dodged, and after a couple more attempts, they'd share a chaste pressing of lips to lips. It wasn't much, but all that Russell dared push for.

She licked the rim of her mug, definitely teas-ing him. "Annette says that a couple of those boys from the lake invited us out to hear a band tomor-row."

"Neat."

Her sardonic eyebrow suggested she'd heard his sarcasm. "It'll be fun, Russell. You're the one who said this was our last chance to play before…"

"Before?" he teased, just to hear what she'd say.

She laughed, pushing against his chest. "Before you get a job and we…"

This time she had the grace to look embarrassed. He hadn't actually proposed to her yet.

"Before we find a little house, maybe one of the new ones out by the new golf club?"

She sat straight up, obviously surprised. "In Red Wing?"

"Well, yeah." He shrugged, puzzled by her reaction. There weren't that many lawyers in town, so he figured they could always use another one.

"But I thought you'd look for something in Minneapolis, or maybe even Chicago."

"Chicago?"

She downed her whiskey, and once she stopped sputtering, her smile was back in place. "Doesn't matter, lamb chop. Wherever you take a job will be just fine."

He took a bite of cookie and nodded, the oatmeal sticking in his mouth. He hated disappointing her, and somehow he had.

She followed his lead, nibbling on the cookie with a sour face. "Oatmeal and whiskey aren't the best combination."

"Nope."

They sat a little farther apart and drank some more whiskey, but Russell no longer wanted to try for a kiss.

## Chapter 3

℀

"THREE MORE LAPS, THEN HEAD back-stage." Russell stood on the deck, fists planted on his hips, the cuffs of his white button-down shirt rolled to just below his elbows.

"Will whoever's closest splash the penguin on the deck?" Susie giggled, sending a small wave in Russell's direction.

Annette jumped at the chance to tease him. "Yeah, cuz. You going to church tonight?"

"Swim, ladies." Russell put some backbone into his tone, more than willing to pull Susie and Annette out of the pool for a quick ten sit-ups if they gave him too much trouble. His aunt had hired him to be the assistant coach, dammit, and he meant to do his best.

Susie took off for her warm-up laps, and with a solid dolphin kick, Annette did the same. Her wave came so close to the hem of his slacks, he had to hop out of the way. He'd never admit it to the girls, but he liked dressing nice for opening night. He had a navy suit jacket stashed in the men's locker, along with a silk tie. Green, for luck.

An hour later, over five thousand people crowded the grandstands to watch the Aqua Dears, the Aqua Darlings, and the divers put on their show against a rose-and-plum sunset, the kind ordained by Hollywood. Even the ducks paddling along the edge of the lake outside the theater seemed impressed.

Russell had staked out a spot at the end of the front row, making notes for later. Aunt Maude watched from the wings, wearing a smart pink dress with pearls around her neck and white gloves. The girls swam well, the crowd loved the show, and Russell was just as impressed by the trumpet solo the second time around.

Afterwards, he found Susie behind the brick building near the edge of the lake. Annette was with her, along with the trumpet player and his short, dark-eyed friend.

"Russell!" Susie squealed when she saw him, excitement tinged with guilt.

"Susie, Annette," he said, standing in a pool of light from the lamp on the corner of the building, while the others were in the shadows near the shore.

Susie introduced him to her new friends Ryker and Skip. "Ryker wants us to go with them to hear a band play, Russ. Do you think we can escape your aunt's clutches?"

Russell didn't move, letting her come to him. She grasped the open edges of his jacket with a conspiratorial wink. Annette had her hands clasped behind her back and her breasts aimed at Skip, the trumpet player.

He dropped an arm around Susie's shoulders, deliberately proprietary. He dared a circumspect glance at Skip, but the trumpet player was staring out over the water. Fair enough. "Sure, Sus. We can meet them after lights out."

A rumble from the direction of the parking lot announced the bus's return.

"You all are staying over at the university, aren't you?" Ryker aimed his question at all of them.

"Yeah, at Hansee Hall," Susie answered.

Ryker raised an eyebrow at Skip.

"I don't know either." Skip shrugged. "I'm not the college boy."

"Forty-fifth and Twentieth," Russell said, earning a half smile from the trumpet player. Annette interrupted them with a giggle and a toss of her hair. Skip appeared interested in her performance, and Russell's little flicker of excitement died as if someone had pinched the wick of a candle. A moment later, his aunt's whistle blast curtailed their conversation.

Annette kept a possessive hand on Skip's arm. "We can meet you somewhere at midnight."

"Walk over to University Avenue," Ryker said.

Skip stepped away from Annette, as casually as if he hadn't noticed her womanly curves. "We'll pick you up."

After a brief flurry of nervous conversation and a second whistle blast, the trio headed to the bus, leaving the musicians behind.

The bus dropped them off about forty-five minutes before one of the chaperones went door-to-door announcing lights out. Russell's dorm room had cove ceilings, stone floors, and the pervasive smell of old soup, and his mattress squealed in pain when he sat down. Next door, his aunt rustled around, and muffled giggles from overhead told him the swimmers were settling in for the night.

Fifteen minutes after lights out, Russell cracked his door open.

He let the girls go first so he could make sure no one heard them leave. He had pulled a couple of bills out of his emergency fund, money he'd earned working for his father's farm supply business over school breaks. He didn't have much, barely enough to tide him over till he landed a job. Which he would do, as soon as he got back from the Aqua Dears' tour.

If he couldn't find anything better, he'd be selling fertilizer again.

In the dormitory's common room, one small table lamp created a pool of light in the corner. A choking snore from the direction of his aunt's room disrupted the heavy quiet. Doubt curled out of the shadows, setting the stage for his internal debate.

After three years of law school, he was very good at defending a position.

Convincing the girls to stay at the dorm would avoid any of the trouble that would trigger his aunt's ire. The opposite side—either the prosecution or defense, he wasn't sure—argued that adventure was the whole reason for making this trip. Sneaking out with Susie for a night of rock 'n' roll was the kind of thing he'd signed up for.

Russell took a moment to review each assertion, then stretched his arms over his head and arched back to work out the kinks in his shoulders and spine. It was an old swimmer's habit, but he wouldn't get a really good stretch until he led the girls in calisthenics in the morning.

The judge ruled in favor of adventure.

If they got busted, he'd be there to keep the girls out of trouble. And if they didn't, well, it'd be worth the risk. Decision made, he listened to the sleeping quiet, excitement percolating through his gut. After giving the girls a five-minute head start, he joined them in the alley.

"This way." He grabbed Susie's hand and Annette's elbow and marched them down to 40th Street. Once they were away from the dormitory, both girls erupted in giggles.

"Russell, you are the most," Annette said. "I like having you as a chaperone."

Russell smirked but didn't respond. Both girls wore narrow trousers and short-sleeved blouses, though Annette's pants were tighter and she'd left a couple of her blouse buttons open. She was the fast one, the kind of girl a guy could take liberties with. Susie barely reached her shoulder, a perfect little green-eyed doll. Her high-heeled pumps lifted her from tiny to just short. They were both pretty enough to turn Russell into a bulldog. They saw fun and adventure where he saw strange men ready to make their move.

"Since you and Susie are jacketed, I get to choose between Skip and Ryker, right?"

Annette's flirtatious giggle got a snort from

Russell.

"Shut up, Annette," Susie said. "Ryker's too short for you anyway."

"You're right. I like tall boys, and Skip's handsome enough. We'll look like a couple of movie stars together."

Unaccountably irritated, Russell picked up the pace, walking so quickly, Susie had to skip to keep up.

University Street was crowded, but an old Buick with a blunt nose and bulging wheel wells pulled up to the curb and flashed its lights. Skip was driving, Annette called dibs on the front seat, and soon Russell, Susie, and Ryker were packed in the back.

In a couple of blocks, the streets quieted, but instead of the rows of boxy houses, Russell's attention was caught on Skip's hair, slicked in place with pomade, the trim curls falling in rows to the back of his neck.

Waiting at a red light, Skip twisted around, catching Russell's eye. "Doing okay?"

*Caught.* Russell's guard went up. Ryker and Susie were hot in a conversation he'd long since given up trying to follow. "Sure. What year is this machine?"

"Nineteen forty-eight." Skip looked him over, making Russell conscious of his rumpled trousers, open jacket, and loosened tie.

Surprise held Russell still for the extended appraisal. He told himself the way Skip chewed on his lower lip wasn't meant to tease, and his slow smile couldn't have been an invitation. He told himself the heat building in his groin would fade away.

The light turned green. Annette turned and bounced onto her knees to check out the back seat.

"Isn't this swell?" she asked, showering them with bright-eyed excitement.

*Swell.* Russell sat straighter and shook his jacket closed. Ryker had an arm draped along the top of the seat, almost but not quite touching Susie, who was explaining the finer points of water ballet, tapping his knee with her index finger for emphasis. Russell shifted again, and the flask in his inner coat pocket rubbed against his ribs. He brought it out, and everyone took a hit, everyone except Skip, who kept his hands on the steering wheel and asked for a rain check.

Russell took a final hit from the flask and put it away, trying not to notice the man's fingers pressing random patterns into the wheel.

"What's your favorite record?" Skip asked, directing his comment to the group.

Susie jumped in first. "'Unchained Melody.'"

"I like Pat Boone," Annette said, which prompted Ryker to blow a raspberry. "What?" she yelped. "He's a wonderful singer."

Ryker mimed a yawn, leaned against the car door, and pretended to sleep.

"I prefer Frank," Russell said. Skip raised an eyebrow but didn't comment.

"He sings just like him," Susie said, pointing to Russell.

Skip shot a glance over his shoulder. "You can sing?"

"He used to be in the Glee Club."

Russell sighed from deep in his gut. "Shut up, Susie."

"What do you mean? You're a great singer." She grabbed his hand and held it, as if by the warmth of her enthusiasm, she could force his secrets out. "He's sung in bands before too, and in school musicals and everything."

"Susie." Russell wrenched his hand away, embarrassment ratcheting another twist to his bowels.

"Maybe we'll see if you can sit in with the band tonight," Ryker said, with just enough of a challenge to set Russell's teeth on edge.

Russell waved him off. "I don't think so." He could carry a tune and find his way around the piano keyboard, but nothing close to what these guys were capable of.

"We've got a little combo," Skip said, putting on the turn signal, his attention on the road. "You could come jam with us one night while you're here."

Both Annette and Susie got so excited about the idea of a jam session that Russell had to concede defeat. "Sure. Some night I'll sing 'Misty' for you."

"It's a date." Skip pulled the car into a parking spot next to a worn-out old building, on a street full of worn-out buildings. "Time to slide on in."

The sly grin accompanying Skip's invitation went straight to Russell's balls. To cover, he made a production out of helping the girls from the car.

A single neon sign marked the doorway to the club, and from the stage, The Enchanters' steady beat thrummed in Russell's veins. The restaurant's tables had all been shoved to the side to make space for dancing, and beer cans, highball glasses, and ashtrays littered every flat surface. Russell cracked his knuckles, fighting the tension that had already started to build. He hated dancing, and back home, he usually let Susie find another partner. In this crowd of strangers, though, he didn't know who he could trust.

Ryker found them a table against the wall, and Annette looked happy enough to burst when a handsome guy in a University of Washington jersey came over and asked her to dance. She gave Skip a flirtatious wink and followed her new partner onto the dance floor.

Russell pulled a chair out for Susie, Skip and Ryker grabbing seats on the opposite side of the table. Susie wrapped her hand around Russell's wrist with a giggle. "I want to dance."

"Come on, Sus." Disentangling himself from her grasp. Russell settled into the chair next to hers.

"No really." She bounced on the balls of her feet. "This band is great."

"I'll…" Ryker braced himself on the table and half rose. "I could—"

Skip elbowed him.

"Knock it off." Ryker shot his friend a mock glare, and he bowed to Susie. "I'll dance with you."

Her eyes got really round. "Is that okay, Russell?"

He took her hand, rubbing her small fingers with his thumb. If this guy did anything bad, he'd know where to find him. "Sure, Susie. Have fun."

Somehow the sight of Ryker's hand on Susie's

shoulder hit Russell like a solid tap to his chest. That sensation was quickly swallowed by the awkwardness of being alone at the table with Skip.

Russell broke a sweat, took his jacket off, draped it over the chair. All around him, couples clung together, groping, laughing, with the occasional press of lips to skin.

He and Skip made an island of silence in the crowd. Skip had on a white short-sleeved jersey and blue jeans, his curly pompadour flopping down over his brow. He smelled clean, unfussy, with enough spice to keep Russell interested. The scent carried over the smell of cigarettes and stale beer.

"Want something to drink?" Russell didn't want to seem rude. Buying everyone a beer was as good a dodge as any.

"Sure."

Skip suggested Rainier, a local brew Russell had never heard of. The trip to the bar didn't take as long as he thought it would, and Susie was still on the dance floor when he returned. Annette stood off to the side with a couple of young men, and Skip seemed content to wait and watch.

"Bottoms up." Russell raised his beer, using the awkward toast to cover his nerves. *Nerves?* Skip hadn't done anything. Russell just didn't trust his own response to the man.

Skip grinned and tapped Russell's beer with his own. "So, you like to sing, and I guess you like to swim. What else do you like to do?"

Ryker swung Susie around, lifting her from the waist. The way she tipped her head and laughed twisted something in Russell's gut.

"I mean, do you like—"

"Geez, I'm sorry." Russell's cheeks heated, embarrassed that he'd ignored Skip's question. He didn't dance. Susie did. He'd watched her before. "I go jogging and sometimes lift weights…generally try to keep fit."

"I can see that." Skip's sideways glance gave him something else to blush over. He would have given anything for the song to end so Susie would come back. Skip's boldness left Russell with very little doubt about where his inclinations lay, and no way was he going to make that mistake again.

"And now that I'm done with school, I like to read." There. See? Nothing flirtatious about reading.

"Me too." Skip's smile broadened. "Who's your favorite author?"

"Let me think." Russell leaned over the table, propped on his elbows. With something safe to talk about, he unwound some. "Hemingway is good, or maybe Salinger."

"Oh-ho. You like the heavy stuff."

Skip's chuckle heated Russell's cheeks again. *Damn.* He shook himself and sat up straighter. "Not really. What do you like to read?"

"Those magazines, you know? The short ones, where you can get twenty Westerns for twenty-five cents, or maybe stories about space aliens or private eyes." Skip rubbed his thumb up and down the beer can, a tiny gesture Russell found distracting.

"I've seen those at the barber shop."

"Do you ever read them?"

"Sure." The band stopped, and Russell looked hopefully in Susie's direction. She and Ryker stayed out on the dance floor.

"You do?"

Russell took a long swallow of his beer and shot Skip a grin. "Nah, but next time I get a haircut, I will." He polished off the rest of the beer. Susie was having way too much fun with Ryker, but short of causing a scene, he didn't know what to do about it.

"I wouldn't mind having another nip off that hard stuff in your flask. Wanna duck outside for a minute?" Skip's expression was open, honest, not hinting at anything at all. Maybe Russell had just overreacted when they first sat down.

He crumpled his beer can and stood up. "Sure."

# Chapter 4

## ℭ

THEIR WALK TO THE PARKING lot gave Skip the chance to admire how Russell's threads molded to his butt and thighs. The bigger man had the body of a Greek god, but it was his shyness that got to Skip. Even though Russell kept a tight hold on that little brunette girl, Skip could tell he got under his skin.

He'd be happy to get under Russell's blue jeans too.

Lou would smack his head for teasing Russell, but Skip couldn't help himself. Lou offered Skip many things: friendship, a decent cover, and the occasional blow job. And reams of advice, good and otherwise.

When Skip had crossed the line into blatant flirting, Russell blushed like a girl. Skip liked the charge that came with pushing the pedal down, and—despite Lou's opinions—he had enough self-preservation to know when to cut the gas.

Skip followed Russell to a shadowy area in the back of the parking lot, and once they were out of sight of anyone in the club, Russell brought out the flask and handed it over. Skip took a hit, the whiskey's smoky burn warming his chest on the way down. "I got another question for you."

Russell took the flask and raised an eyebrow.

"How come you don't dance?" Skip was mainly curious, but the words carried more heat than he'd intended.

Russell snorted, crossing his arms over his chest in a way that made his biceps bulge. "I just don't."

"Maybe you need someone to teach you." Lou would sure scold him for this one. "Maybe you just need the right person."

Russell's fists clenched, and for half a second, Skip thought he might haul off and punch him. Heck, he probably deserved it. Then Russell choked out a laugh. "The right person. Sure."

"I mean…" Since he hadn't been served a knuckle sandwich, Skip struck a pose, hip cocked, hands in the air like they were on a partner's shoulders. "I can do the cha-cha." He swung his hips, fighting a laugh at Russell's perplexed expression. "Or the swing." He mimed a four-step pattern, then swung his hips again for good measure. Russell appeared transfixed by the motion.

A shout of laughter distracted them. A group of people spilled out the nightclub's door, a woman's voice rising over the hubbub. "Where are we going again?"

Russell shifted in their direction, hands on his hips. "Annette?" he said softly.

"Wait. I want to go back in and hear the band." To Skip's ear, the woman wasn't laughing nearly as hard as the bunch of guys she was with.

"Come on, sugar. It's just out here," one of the men said. Skip didn't like the way he laughed.

"No."

This time there was no mistaking the distress in her voice. Russell took off running, with Skip right behind. He detoured to the door of the club, where he ran into Ryker and Susie. They were laughing, his arm around her shoulder.

"Come on, you guys," Skip said. "It sounds like your friend Annette's in some trouble."

By the time they got to the other end of the parking lot, Russell was chest to chest with a drunken college boy, the kind with pale skin, a buzz cut, and a mean attitude. Skip looked around for anything he could use as a weapon if it came to a fight. There were two other fellows backing the one in front of Russell, and Annette huddled against a car, tears streaking her cheeks.

"So you're going to take on all three of us? All by your lonesome?" The boy stuck his finger in Russell's chest. Russell grabbed his wrist and leaned into him. The college boy was taller, but Russell was broader and bulkier.

"If I have to."

Under different circumstances, the rock-solid certainty in Russell's tone would have given Skip a hard-on. Saving that thought for later, he grabbed a thick branch lying between the cars.

"One against three." Another of the college boys snickered.

Skip stepped forward, holding the branch loosely. "Looks like three against three to me." Ryker followed his lead.

One of the arrogant fools came right up to Ryker. "Two and a half against three, I'd say."

With a click, Ryker opened a switchblade. "Funny how this extends my reach."

Swinging the branch, Skip took a step forward. The college boys all shifted back, even the one facing off with Russell. Skip might be slender and a little light in his boots, but anyone who grew up in Pioneer Square knew how to fight. He and Ryker moved into position on either side of Russell, and the college boys backed off.

"We were just playing anyway." One of them laughed like it was all a joke.

"Didn't sound like that to me," Russell said. "I think you should apologize to my cousin."

"Your cousin's a slut."

Skip wasn't sure which one said it, but before anyone could respond, Russell took three big steps forward and put his fist into the middle guy's belly. The boy dropped to his knees, and Russell stood over him. "Anyone else?"

The other two beat feet, which didn't surprise Skip. These candy-ass college boys were all show and no go. Susie ran up to Annette, with Russell right behind her. "I'm going to get the car," Skip said to Ryker. "We gotta cut out."

In a matter of minutes, they were packed into Skip's Buick, Russell and Susie in the rear seat with Annette between them. Annette had shifted from crying to spitting mad, and Skip felt like he should apologize, though he wasn't quite sure for what. Russell, Susie, and Annette were guests in his town, and he didn't want them to be scared to come out with him and Ryker.

As they backed out of the parking spot, motion caught his eye. Russell, flexing and flaring his hand.

"You okay?" Skip asked. He'd landed a solid punch.

Russell didn't answer, except for a slight shrug. Skip held his gaze for longer than was probably safe. Held his gaze, and wanted.

*Who am I kidding?* He just hoped Russell would agree to do something—anything—after tomorrow night's show. Lou was going to kill him, but Skip couldn't help his feelings. As long as he stayed clear of the law, he was willing to roll the dice.

**❧**

"Did you see how long Blondie's legs are?" Ryker asked. He took a lazy drag off his cigarette, stretching back against the big bench seat of Skip's Buick. They were headed for a late-night rehearsal with their jazz combo. Two nights had passed since they'd gone to see The Enchanters, and Russell had been making himself scarce.

Skip flipped the turn signal and tapped the brake. The swimmers were splotches of color from the stage and the source of the water splashing on his back while he played. He regarded girls as a generally affable part of his reality, sometimes pretty, sometimes funny, sometimes smart. They were painted with big bright brushes, while the men he knew stood out, all detail, energy, and heat. "Which one?"

"The one that came with us the other night… Amanda? Alice? Something starting with an A."

"Annette." Skip kept his chin pointed at the front window, but inside, he was shaking his head. Ryker only really paid attention to the women he wanted to bed.

"Annette." Ryker rolled down the car window. "She's your type."

Skip waited for oncoming traffic to clear before he turned left onto North 45th Street, doing his best not to snort out loud. "Really?"

"She's the same as your friend Lulu, you know, leggy and loud." Ryker spiked his cigarette butt at the street. "If you'd asked her to dance, we could have avoided a lot of trouble."

These conversations didn't happen very often, and when they did, Skip tried not to let it rattle his cage. "So it was all my fault."

"I don't mean it like that." Ryker shrugged apologetically. "Now Lulu's a fox, but since she's not coming around anymore, you should find someone new."

They made the left turn and wound their way through the Wallingford neighborhood, heading toward Northlake Street. Ryker's father owned an old warehouse down on a stretch of Lake Union between shipbuilders and the Seattle Gas Light Company's coal ossification plant.

The warehouse's manager knew Skip and Ryker and allowed them to use the space for rehearsal, as long as they didn't fool with the merchandise. Somewhere along the line, someone had brought in an upright piano. The cement floor made it hard to hear each other, and the damp air made it impossible to keep the piano in tune, but the space was free and there were no neighbors to complain about the noise.

"Why did you break up with Lulu anyway?" Ryker shifted in his seat, giving Skip his full attention. "Did she step out on you? Find another guy?"

"In a manner of speaking." Skip stifled a smirk. Lou owned more pairs of stiletto heels than any three women. Every so often, Ryker insisted on a double date, and when Lou set his hair and put on lipstick and a string of pearls, only someone looking for a queen would figure it out. Skip and Lou hadn't been an official couple since high school, but even then they'd been held together by shared secrets more than anything else.

Skip's taste ran toward more manly men. Men who wouldn't back down from a fight. Men who were strong enough to blush.

"Well, if you don't want what Annette's cooking"—Ryker's grin was begging for trouble—"you can eyeball some of the other girls."

"What other girls?" Skip pressed a palm against his temple where frustration was pinging like Woody Woodpecker on a pole. "We're having band practice, right? Just us and the guys, right?"

"I told you I found us dates."

*Crap.* "Who else did you invite?"

"Susie's going to ask Annette and a few of the others, and I expect her bodyguard will be there too."

*Russell.* Skip flipped, excitement buzzing in his belly. "But Paddy and Todd expect to rehearse." Those woodpecker pings turned into a headache. Skip had been looking forward to playing something low-key after a week pretending to be first chair in Glenn Miller's band.

Ryker straightened the collar of his black leather jacket. "Told them to invite people too. Paddy's bringing beer, and we can drag out the piano and the drum kit so if people want to jam, they can."

Gripping the wheel at ten and two o'clock, Skip mulled over the party idea. He didn't have to turn on the jets to figure out why Russell had been avoiding him. Though Skip couldn't imagine flirting with Annette, or any other girl, maybe it was time for him to start playing it cool.

# Chapter 5

❦

A LOGICAL MAN WOULD AVOID DANGER, and Russell had always prided himself on his ability to take a rational approach to any situation. But every night at the lake, the sweet sound of Skip's trumpet seared his soul, so when Susie insisted they drop in on the band's jam session, he hadn't resisted. Instead, he sat in the back of a ramshackle cab, his arm around Susie's shoulders, letting himself be carried along by her excitement.

Though his resolve rang hollow right now, he had every intention of making Susie happy for the rest of her life.

The cab dropped them off in front of a grotty old warehouse about a mile and a half from any signs of life. Streetlights marked the end of every block, but neither of the closest two gave off enough light to reach the warehouse in the middle. If it weren't for the strip of light underneath a door at the far end of the building and the occasional splash of a cymbal, Russell would have chased their cab down and taken the girls back to the dorm.

Until he was sure of the situation, he made the

girls stand behind him and slowly opened the door. Everyone inside turned in their direction. Ryker and another man were rolling a piano across the floor. Skip stood in a doorway in the back, carrying a kick drum. Shadows hid his expression, and after locating the man, Russell kept his gaze anywhere else. A couple of other fellows were seated on stools. One held a dinged-up trombone and the other held a can of beer.

Even worse, three other Aqua Dears stood in a cluster between the men on stools, holding on to beers too.

His aunt was going to skin him alive.

"Hey, Jenny." Annette swanned across the room like a debutante at a grand ball. "How'd you guys get down here?"

Susie skipped along behind Annette, Russell scrambling to keep hold of her hand. The warehouse had a cement floor and dim corners, stacks of boxes, and metal brackets suspended from the ceiling. Silver metal fixtures hung down in a row, and under their harsh white light, Russell took stock of everyone. Skip, Ryker, and their friends were hipsters, and next to their rolled-up dungarees and slicked-back hair, Russell felt like an oddball. His khakis still had a pleat, for chrissake.

The main door banged open, and more people came in. Pretty soon there were twenty-five or thirty young people hanging out drinking beer. Some had instruments, playing a disorganized mix of horn riffs and guitar chords and plunking bass notes.

"This is the best." Susie's squeal caught his attention. "Are you going to sing with them?"

Russell took a nip from the flask in his pocket. He couldn't afford to get drunk, but he needed something to take the edge off. "I don't know. Maybe."

"You have to. Come on. Let's go talk to Skip and Ryker." She tugged on his hand, and after a brief, futile attempt to dig in his heels, he followed. All the way across the warehouse floor, his internal debate ran on. Sitting in with the band would make Susie happy, but making a fool of himself in front of a bunch of fellows who could really play, well…

But why did he care? He'd be gone in a week. He did care, though. Skip's presence was like a bright light at the edge of his vision, something he couldn't quite ignore. His voice, his laughter, a half glimpse of his lean torso bending over to lift a guitar drove Russell near to distraction. *Stop it.* Russell's own nature might be twisted and depraved, but his rational mind made the decisions.

His decision had been made a long time ago.

As they approached the musicians, the smile on Susie's heart-shaped face both warmed and reassured Russell. They shook hands all around, and before Russell could stop her, Susie had dragged him to the center of the group.

"Russell's a great piano player."

He shook his head at her. His mother had ensured he had a passing acquaintance with Chopin, but that was it. "Susie."

"Hey, we're just having fun here tonight." Skip's smile was friendly, without any added innuendo.

Since he couldn't back down without making a fool of himself, Russell approached the piano and raised the cover. The ivories were worn, some of them mottled with brown, as familiar as his own face. He sank onto the stool's leather-padded seat, checked the height, stood to screw the seat down a couple of inches. Then he got himself comfortable and ran his hands over the keys.

On impulse, he played the opening measures of Beethoven's Minuet in G. He wanted a sense of the instrument's tone and tuning. Instead, he got booed.

"Don't be a drip," someone shouted from across the room. "Play some Monk."

"Perry Como," came from someone else.

"Panty waist."

With shouts and laughter carrying him along, Russell scrambled for a song to play, until Susie's voice caught is attention.

"Play that song," she said.

*That song*…by Frank Sinatra. *That song*… he could sing while he played. *That song*…he'd learned because it was her favorite. "I've Got the World on a String." He ran a scale, let his fingers find the opening notes. Twangy. He made a face. Brash tone.

Well, his voice was twangy and brash too.

"Be quiet," Ryker yelled from somewhere behind Russell's right shoulder. Russell paused, wondering if he should give over the instrument to someone else.

Ryker knocked his arm a little too hard. "Not you. I can already tell you're bona fide."

Russell didn't want to overdo things, so he caught Skip's eye. "You sing? I'm pretty good at transposing. We can find a song and a key—"

"Nah, man. I wanna hear your sounds."

Russell shrugged, ran through the opening chords, and started to sing.

The lyrics were nonsense, his delivery nowhere near Frank Sinatra's casual cool, but there was scattered applause. Squealing from Susie. Conversation faded and left him holding the weight of everyone's attention. He had no microphone, his voice was husky from barking at the girls during their warm-up, and the lyrics pounded on his uncertainty.

It was, after all, a song about being in love.

Susie's arms circled his neck, startling him into a gasp. Her soft floral scent relaxed him. She nuzzled his shoulder, and he breathed a little deeper, steadying his voice for the end of the verse.

A snare drum joined in, tapping the beat when he got to the bridge. The second time through the verse, he stopped singing and let the piano swing for eight bars or so, pulling back when a horn chimed in on the melody.

The thought of jamming with the trumpet player tightened him up again, but it was a saxophone, not a trumpet; some other guy, not Skip. The impromptu ensemble came back to the bridge, and on instinct, the band pulled back so his voice could be heard.

Another horn, maybe a clarinet, grabbed the melody, and a trombone seconded the rolling baseline in Russell's left hand. They kept it up, trading leads, and at some point, a string bass joined in. Russell pulled back further, comping along with the horn players, just a silly so-and-so in the band. After the sixth repeat, he raised one hand to cue the others to the last verse.

Russell all but shouted the first words of the line and pointed at the drummer, who roared into the break. Another short phrase, then a high horn, the clarinet or a soprano sax, played a fierce, bluesy trill. The last phrase, a declaration. *I'm in love.*

Well? Was he? Just asking the question made him flush.

Applause and laughter. Cheers and stomping on the floor. Susie gave him a big slobbery kiss on the cheek. Ryker knocked him on the back again. "From now on, I'm calling you Frank."

Russell brushed him off and half stood. Skip pointed at the stool and shook his head. "You're not done yet, buddy. You know any Louis Jordan?"

A guitar plucked a melody.

"Maybe?" Russell said.

Skip put a hand on his shoulder. "Well, we're going to teach you to improvise, then. Paddy, you count us off."

The bass player hoisted his oversized cello and stood where Russell could hear him call out the chord changes. They jammed on the tune for a while, then someone called out another one, and they kept going.

Russell didn't know all the tunes, but no one seemed to care, so pretty soon he stopped caring too. He relaxed and laughed and just had fun.

During a break between songs, Skip leaned

against the piano keyboard. "You promised you'd sing 'Misty' for us, Russ."

"Did I?" Russell scratched his head, grinning at the keys. "I don't think I can sing it and play at the same time."

"Don't worry about it. What key?"

They worked out the details, and Skip strutted over to the guitar player. The band started up, a little rough around the edges, and Russell sang. The words were hokey, and Skip's smile got to him. And Skip's horn? The sound wrapped around his heart and squeezed.

Several songs later, Russell had exhausted his musical capacity and yielded the piano. "You guys are set to jam all night," he said, waving off the musician's protests, "and I have to find my girl."

"Do what you got to do," Skip said with a distracted smile.

Russell stood, stretched, and glanced around the room. Where were Susie and the others? Grabbing a beer and a place on the sidelines, he scanned the crowd. It didn't take him long to find all the swimmers, all of them except his girlfriend.

During a break between songs, someone banged through the main door. "The heat," they yelled. "Circled the block twice now."

*Shoot.* If he and the other Aqua Dears got arrested, Aunt Maude would string him up. He didn't know about the laws in Seattle, but back home, drinking beer in an old warehouse could get them in a whole lot of trouble. He waved at Annette, intending to ask her to round up the others, when Skip bumped him. Hard.

"Here." Skip shoved keys into Russell's hand. "You can drive, right? Get the girls. We gotta get outa here."

Russell nodded, and Skip kept moving. He went to the next closest cluster of people, and Russell waved Annette over. "Did you hear that?"

"I wasn't listening." She shrugged.

"The police are outside. Get everyone together and meet me at Skip's car."

"Oh shoot." For once, Annette's poise seemed to fail her. "What are you going to do?"

"Look for Susie."

"Oh."

Her brows closed in, taking her expression from nervous to scared, but Russell didn't have time for her dramatics. "Just find the others."

Annette scurried off, and Russell made a big circuit of the room.

Susie was nowhere around.

*Dammit.*

The crowd quickly faded away, and the yoke of responsibility chafed, weighed him down. Fear and anger duked it out in his belly. *Where the hell is she?* He headed for the door at a jog. The warehouse was empty. She wasn't inside. She must be hiding in some dark corner where the streetlights didn't reach. Russell planned to start with a lap of the building, then take his search around the block if he needed to.

Annette caught him before he'd crossed the threshold. "Now promise you won't be mad."

"What?"

She attempted to block him, but over her shoulder, he saw Ryker came around the corner of the building, holding Susie around the waist. She had an arm draped over his shoulders and was obviously tipsy.

"Hey, Annette." She staggered; not just tipsy, she was flat-out drunk. Losing her balance, she caught herself on Ryker. "Hey, come back here and help me. That's a good boy."

One hand pressed flat to Ryker's chest, and her body stretched against him in a surprisingly intimate way. Russell froze, unable to think of anything to say.

Annette strode over to the couple, heels clicking on the asphalt. "Come on, Sus. It's time to go."

Susie held her index finger to her lips. "Shh. Don't tell anybody, but Ryker's a really good kisser." She erupted in giggles, even as Annette dragged her away.

Surprise muffled his thinking, but as it faded, Russell's chest hurt as if he'd had the wind knocked out of him. Embarrassment fueling his anger, he caught Ryker's eye. He straightened to his full height, debating whether he should punch the guy out. Or rather, weighing the costs of teaching the guy a lesson.

From behind him, fingers grasped his arm. Skip. "Can you help me out here?"

Russell turned his head slowly, without letting go of Ryker's gaze. "What?"

"We need to stow the gear so the manager doesn't get hacked off." Skip's grip was firm enough to let him know he wouldn't be punching anyone.

He inhaled hard, jaw so tight he could have cracked a tooth. He was outnumbered, and he knew it. "Yeah, okay."

"Paddy will take Annette and the others as far as Forty-fifth and University Street. We can meet them there."

Skip's voice held just enough sympathy to let Russell know he wasn't completely outnumbered. "Wait, you know the manager? Why are we leaving, then?"

"Because Ryker's dad will be cranked if he finds out the cops had to shut down a party out here."

Russell followed Skip back into the warehouse, and together they shoved the piano in a shallow alcove off the main floor. They moved the drum kit without taking it apart and picked up as many beer cans as they could find in five minutes or less.

"If you want," Skip said, dumping an armload of empties in a trash can. "How about tomorrow after the show, you and me go out for a drink."

Russell paused in his reach for a can. "I'm not sure…"

"I mean"—Skip held his hands with the palms open—"you just look like you could use a friend."

A friend. Since leaving college, Russell hadn't seen many of his friends.

"Think about it, anyway," Skip said. He was over by the wall with his hand on a toggle. He flipped the switch. The big overhead lights went out.

Russell stood at the top of the long rectangle made by moonlight through the front door. Everyone was gone. The quiet pressed against his ears and amplified the blood thrumming through his veins. "Sure."

"Go out to the car, and I'll lock up." Skip's voice came from the direction of the light switch, softer, huskier than normal. The moment stretched out, strangely intimate. He cleared his throat. "Go on now."

Still, Russell didn't move, locked in a battle between doing the correct thing, the expected thing, and the one thing he wanted to do. His fists clenched, knuckles jammed into his thighs. He did not need to get back at Susie by messing around with Skip.

"Go," Skip whispered.

Russell went.

☾

Skip looped the heavy padlock through the hook in the doorjamb, kicking himself for letting Ryker throw a party. Although, if he were honest, he'd own that Russell's turn with the band was worth some trouble. Skip wouldn't have predicted the poolside god could have done such a fine job with a Frank Sinatra tune.

A car door slammed. Russell must have made it back to the Buick. He loped over to the car and flung open the passenger door. Two of the swimmers were in the back, with Russell in the passenger seat, his khaki pants rumpled and his normally smooth cheeks showing the hint of a shadow.

"Slide over," Skip said.

"Why?"

"You can drive, right?" This wasn't the time to admit how much he liked the idea of having a tough guy drive his car.

Russell nodded with a grimace.

Skip shrugged, fighting to keep the tease out of his grin. "You've got the keys."

Russell's answering smile was more tired than anything else, but he slid across the seat and grasped the steering wheel. Skip climbed in, Russell turned the key, and the engine rumbled, a rich, dirty sound vibrating through Skip's solar plexus.

"Make a right out of the parking lot," Skip said, *and drive that baby right over here.* Russell had a hand on the gearshift, but the flashing blue light of a police car pulled in behind them.

"Shoot," Skip said. He glanced over his shoulder, blinking into the cop car's headlights. "Ryker's dad's going to be hacked."

"Russell," one of the girls in the back squeaked, "we're going to get into trouble."

"It'll be all right, Phyllis."

He said it with so much confidence, even Skip believed him.

The police officer's bulky form approached, a wide black belt slung under his generous belly. "You've got your license with you, right?" Skip asked.

The other man gave him a *don't be silly* look. At least Skip hoped his raised eyebrow meant something.

With another long glance at Skip, Russell rolled down the window. The cop flashed a light in the car.

"Officer," Russell said, holding out his license.

The cop tipped the flashlight up, giving Skip

a start. In the semidarkness, he recognized Murphy, a copy whose usual beat was down in Pioneer Square. He and Officer Murphy knew each other pretty well, and Skip eased back against the door, heart pinging in staccato bursts. If he did nothing else, he needed to stay out of the light.

Officer Murphy shone the flashlight on Russell's license. "What's a guy from Red Wing doing out here?"

"Seafair."

Good. The fewer words the better.

Murphy flashed the light around the car again. Skip kept his gaze out the passenger window. The light passed him, then came back.

"Oh, this is good," Murphy laughed. "Mister, um…" Murphy took another glance at the license. "Mr. Haunreiter, what are you doing with a pervert like Skip Johansen?" Another laugh, meaner, nastier. "And who you got back here? Are you two lezzies?"

"Russell." Another plaintive cry came from the girl in the back.

"Excuse me, Officer, but as Mr. Johansen's legal counsel," Russell spoke with more poise than Skip could ever hope for, "may I remind you slander is a crime, and unless you want to charge us with anything, I suggest you go back to your car and let us go."

Murphy's look of surprised dismay made Skip's lips twitch.

"You really a lawyer?" Murphy clearly didn't believe what he'd heard.

Russell met his gaze squarely. "Yes, sir."

Murphy flipped the license onto Russell's lap. "You all go home. It's too late to be hanging around down here." He tucked the flashlight under his armpit and notched his fists on his hips. "And be careful about who you're hanging out with."

The passengers in the Buick stayed silent till the cop car pulled away, then Skip met Russell's gaze and held it.

"You really a lawyer?"

Even Russell's half-assed grin was hotter than anything he'd seen in a good long time. "Close enough."

# Chapter 6

## ₡

THE NEXT MORNING, RUSSELL STOOD shivering on a platform above a crowd of people who were watching the outboard championships on Green Lake. Low-slung, ten-foot hydroplanes buzzed around a loop like a pack of angry lawn mowers, the sound's intensity amplified as it bounced off the orderly Craftsman houses bordering the lake. The swimmers and dancers were surrounded by a raucous, snarling bunch of Seafair Pirates, men of varying ages dressed in shabby costumes spewing humor and abuse. Russell locked a pleasant expression in place till it hurt, suspicious the pirates had authentic grog in their flasks and not some tinted water substitute.

If they were willing to share, he might warm up, though even if the skies cleared and the drizzle stopped, he'd still be in a foul-weather mood.

One of the buccaneers jumped on stage, knocking the Aqua Dears askew. Russell got an arm around Susie's waist before she tipped over the side.

"Thanks." She settled back on her heels. "Almost gave the crowd a real show." Patting at her lemon-yellow skirt, she made a face. "This color is awful enough without showing everybody my undies."

Russell gritted his teeth and nodded as she whined about the outfit and his aunt, the noisy pirates and the noisier hydroplanes, a forcible distraction from reliving the evening before. He shrugged a couple of times to loosen the tension spiraling through his shoulders. Susie might be acting like she couldn't remember anything, but he sure did.

"Come on, ladies, look happy," Aunt Maude hollered from her spot near the front. "You want these nice people to buy tickets to our show, don't you?"

"Not especially," Susie muttered. She smoothed her skirt, her movements tense and jagged.

"Now come on," he said.

The swimmers and dancers giggled and fussed, their matching circle skirts splashing yellow against the overcast sky. The air was so cool, Russell had to wonder why the organizers called this a summertime event.

When things quieted down between races, Susie stood on tiptoe and whispered in Russell's ear. Her words came out as a ticklish blur.

He kept an arm around her waist, holding the platform's wooden railing with the other. "What did you say?"

The boats' grinding drone rose in pitch as they rounded the back turn and headed toward shore. She mumbled something else, and he tipped his head, questioning her with a glance. She pulled on him till they were facing each other. "I said…"

She spoke slowly, emphasizing the words so he couldn't avoid them. "I don't think we should date anymore."

Stunned, Russell loosened his grasp on her ribs. Around them, the crowd gasped as if they'd heard her, though really one of the hydroplanes had flipped. Russell knew how the driver felt. Susie's words caught him by surprise, her meaning caught him far off guard, and her eyes pleaded with him. "Now don't make a scene."

"I won't." He eased away from her. "I'm sorry that you feel that way."

"It's for the best."

He had to work to keep his expression neutral. Though he automatically lined up arguments against her decision, his pride wouldn't allow him to engage her in debate. By ending things in the middle of a crowd, she'd guaranteed that. "I'm sure it is." His pride also wouldn't allow him to take her back. That certainty settled over him, weighing him down.

As if he'd heard Susie's surprise announcement, one of the pirates aimed his squirt gun at them. Susie squealed and ducked behind Russell, and the blast plastered his sport shirt to his chest. Grateful for the excuse, he caught his aunt's eye, gestured to his wet shirt, and left the stage.

Long steps turned into a jog and then a hard run. Russell's oxfords weren't built for it, but he needed the exertion more than he needed to keep his shoes clean. Cruising right past the bus, Russell headed for the road, uncaring which direction was the right one. He turned right, or maybe left, and settled into a steady, hard pace. The light traffic offset his heavy heart, but there was no way he'd outpace the emptiness at the pit of his stomach.

Two years. She'd waited out his last two years of law school, then thrown him over for some little greaser she'd known for a handful of days. Russell's wet shirt slapped against his chest, and a blister started on his right heel, the familiar burn a welcome distraction. He kept running till exhaustion blotted out the shock. By the time he limped back to the dorm, guilt colored his bellyful of sadness. Guilt because he couldn't be the boy Susie wanted, and another helping for his unaccountable relief.

But what the hell am I going to tell Mom?

### ❧

"You can't just leave." Standing under the beam of a parking lot light, Maude tossed the clipboard back to Russell. She sported her usual poodle-do topknot, her flowered dress resembled green Jell-O with fruit in it, and she tried to herd him onto the school bus with the power of her glare.

"I'm looking for somebody." Russell had decided to accept Skip's invitation, and he was damned if he'd let his aunt stop him now. He raised both hands, willing her to calm down. "I'll be right back."

"We need to talk about the opening number first. Your girlfriend lost track of the beat, or didn't you notice?"

Russell straightened his favorite tie, all but choking on his exasperation. The girls seemed to know he and Susie were done, but no one had given Aunt Maude the memo. After two days of pretending things were fine, he was going crazy to talk to someone who wouldn't care. "So did Carole and Betty. I couldn't honestly tell which one of them pulled the others off." Several musicians slunk out behind him, heading into the parking lot, which made keeping his eyes on his aunt almost impossible. A muggy overcast thickened the air, but at least he could claim his sweat was caused by the heat and not by the nerves flapping around his chest like bats in an old barn.

"Maybe you're the one who should talk to her." Aunt Maude pinched her lips together as if it took physical effort not to say something nastier. "Right." She pointed at him. "You tell her she needs to get on the stick."

Skip picked that moment to walk by, sending tension zinging up Russell's spine. His aunt drew a breath to launch another harangue, but he stopped her with a sharp nod. "Fine. I'll talk to Susie." He took a few steps backward, distracted.

"Wait, where are you going?"

"I told you, I'm meeting someone. I'll see you in the morning." He was twenty-three, old enough to find his own way back to the dorm.

"I'm not sure…"

He didn't hang around to hear what she wasn't sure about.

The Buick was parked in the back corner of the lot. Skip set his trumpet in the trunk, locked the tailgate, and climbed in. Russell stopped by the passenger door, pleased by his shadowy reflection in the window. Dark suit coat over a crisp white button-down shirt and neatly trimmed hair; though there were many ways he could fail this test, appearance wouldn't be one of them.

Still, Skip made him wait until the school bus rumbled past in a flash of red lights and overloaded gears. When they were alone, Russell wiped the sweat from his forehead with his handkerchief, stifled the nervous bats in his belly, and opened the door.

"Howdy, stranger," Skip said.

Russell rested his forearms on the roof of the car, his gaze drawn to the black slacks hugging Skip's thighs. "Does your offer for a drink still stand?"

"Sure." Skip raked a hand through the curls dropping over his brow. "We can go down to the Square."

Russell dropped into the seat, smiling to cover the jitters. "Thanks."

Skip loosened the narrow black bow tie that all the musicians wore and tossed it into the backseat. Russell fought the urge to chew on a fingernail, crack his knuckles, or otherwise twitch in his seat.

"Nice of Susie to let you off the chain for tonight." Skip gunned the engine, his sly smile half-cocked in Russell's direction.

Anger threatened to derail him, so Russell drew in a sharp breath, forcing himself to calm down. "Susie and I broke up."

Skip hit the brakes. "Really?"

"Listen." Russell gave up and forced his right fist into his left palm, satisfied by the rat-a-tat pops. "Let's not talk about it, okay. Let's talk about…" Russell scrambled for something innocuous. "Does it ever warm up in this town? It feels like early spring back home."

"The weather?" Easing the car out of the parking lot, Skip flipped the hair out of his eyes with a wide grin. "You're going out for a drink with a new friend, and you want to talk about the weather?"

Russell barked a laugh, overcome by a reckless sense of joy. He'd been holding his cards so close for so long, even this little bit of freedom damned near made him giddy. "All right, then. I put myself in your hands."

"Please."

They both laughed. Skip kept a lazy grip on the wheel, guiding the big car to their mystery destination. Russell relaxed against the cracked vinyl seat and shot shy glances in his direction. He knew he was doing wrong, but couldn't help himself. With every *aw shucks* smile, Skip worked his way further under Russell's skin.

They talked about music and musicians, driving through downtown Seattle and into an older neighborhood, close to the ocean. The streets were lined with worn shops, brick apartments, and rooming houses. Taverns seemed to mark every corner of every block, and the streets were crowded, mostly with men who looked even more worn out than the buildings around them.

The roughness of the neighborhood tightened Russell's anxiety till he could almost hear the whine in the back of his head, high-pitched and brilliant.

Skip parked the car on a side street near the

water and opened the car door, as relaxed as if they were going into church. "Let's agitate the gravel."

The road was paved with cobblestones, and the air smelled of saltwater, roasted peanuts, and piss. Russell turned his ankle on his first step out of the car. He clutched the door handle, managing to keep himself upright.

"Most guys down here have to drink a bit before they start falling down." Skip's tone was dry enough to make Russell wonder if he was joking or not. All around them were the kind of men who drank a bit before they got out of bed, if they even had beds to sleep in.

Russell brushed himself off, straightened to his full height, and edged closer to Skip. If any of these derelicts tried to make trouble, he'd show them how a Midwest boy could fight. "Where are we, anyway?"

"This is First Avenue." Skip nodded at the busy road ahead of them. "Off there"—he pointed to a triangular patch of grass on the left—"is Pioneer Place."

Out on the main street, the city blurred, as big and busy as Minneapolis, much bigger and busier than Red Wing. Black cars crawled along the cobblestone streets like chrome-trimmed insects. The sidewalks were busy; flashy Negro men in cuffed trousers and jewel-tone jackets, drunk and dirty vagrants clustered in empty doorways, and glossy women whose profession was painted in bright red lipstick and short skirts.

Skip strolled through the crowd, seemingly oblivious to the potential for danger. He smiled and nodded at the lowlifes and the winos, and it was all Russell could do to keep his fists shoved into the pockets of his trousers.

A wrought-iron pergola dominated the little square Skip had called Pioneer Place. Opposite the pergola, a totem pole rose twenty feet in the air. Right above the pole, a large neon sign advertised the Seattle Hotel. A light shone from below, highlighting the landmark's weird bird and animal carvings.

Sweat rolled down the small of Russell's back, the result of the humidity, his tension, and his proximity to another man. Skip's self-confidence prodded at Russell, challenged him. Russell prided himself on his honesty, but right then, he was happy not to be on the witness stand. If the judge asked him why he'd agreed to Skip's invitation, no way could he have told the truth.

"You know, back home, people think you all live in teepees out here."

"Well, it's not New York, but this is a city." Skip's brash grin drew an answering smile from Russell. "The mayor and his cronies try to dress things up and call the whole neighborhood Pioneer Square." His fingers brushed Russell's sleeve. "But it'll always be Skid Road. You can pretty much buy anything down here, but you might just lose your shirt doing it if you aren't careful."

Russell stuffed his hands into his trouser pockets. "You're the one who doesn't seem to notice we're surrounded by hoodlums."

"Come on," Skip said, poking him in the chest with a whisper of a wink. "I won't let anything bad happen." He tried to poke a second time, but Russell skittered away. "Besides, no one's going to mess with a big strong boy like you."

"So if there's a fight, then"—Russell gently bumped Skip with his shoulder—"you stand aside and let me win it."

"Hey, now. My mother taught me not to boast." Skip punched him in the arm.

He could have caught him in a wrestling move right there. "I'm not boasting."

"That's right." Skip's laugh was quick and appealing. "I've seen you fight before, big boy."

They walked along the edge of the triangular park, past an old blind man selling peanuts from a cart, and along Second Avenue, where they passed a surprising number of men dressed in business suits and ties. Skip shook hands with a few of them, and Russell felt even more intimidated.

They passed women too, as ordinary as the men in business suits, mingling with the drunks and beggars. Russell had suspicions about one pair of women who walked along beside them a ways before disappearing into a small nightclub.

"In here?" he asked, gesturing toward the club's door.

"Nah, the girls would kill us." Skip again used that dry, half-joking tone. "It's there."

They approached the battered doorway. A short, swarthy man stepped aside to let them in. "Lawrence," he said, wrapping Skip in a back-thumping hug.

"Lawrence?" Russell asked.

Skip ignored him and kept walking into a long,

narrow room. Booths were crowded along one wall across from a heavy marble bar. Heavy curtains covered the windows, blocking out the view of the street.

Somewhere a radio played a stripped-down version of "Caravan." Before they'd gone too far, an older, big-bellied man greeted Skip with an over-affectionate kiss on the cheek. Surprise yanked a gasp from him before he could stop it, and Russell looked around to see if he should be embarrassed.

No one cared. All the customers were men.

# Chapter 7

&

THE TAVERN WAS COMFORTABLE, WARM, touched with the familiar scents of fries and stale beer. Skip waved to acquaintances, amused by the swell of interest in Russell. This place had a select clientele, and if Demetrio the doorman didn't recognize someone, they weren't getting in.

If the characters in this bar were Skip's extended family, then Demetrio was his favorite uncle.

He claimed a booth and tipped his head in the direction of the bartender.

"Lawrence?" Russell dropped onto the seat across from him, chin cocked like he was ready to take a punch.

Over the years, Skip had learned how to balance a friendly smile with a steely attitude, so he rarely ran into trouble on the street, but he sure liked this bulldog side of Russell. He flashed him a grin meant to reassure. "You could take your jacket off, at least."

Russell unwound enough reach for his buttons.

Leaning forward on his forearms, Skip was amused and a little concerned. "Don't make too much of a show, or you'll have half the guys in here offering to help."

Russell loosened his tie with a smile that gave Skip hope. He'd come on strong, maybe too strong, but his date hadn't run. Worth a shot to see where things would go. He really wanted to know what kind of man sat on the other side of the table.

Maybe a little teasing would loosen Russell up. "Do you always dress like a lawyer?"

"Do I?" Russell gave an awkward laugh and shrugged out of his jacket. "Guess I'm just practicing." He paused when the bartender approached them. "Whiskey?"

"I'll have one too."

The grizzled old bartender laid down cocktail napkins and let them alone.

"So what kind of place is this, anyway?" Russell asked. The vibration of his shaking knee traveled under the table, though his hands rested quietly.

"The kind of place where no one asks your last name," Skip said. "And if you stare at someone too long, they're likely to take you out back and get down on their knees." He stifled a grin at the color staining Russell's cheeks. The boy from Red Wing knew what Skip was trying to say, all right. "Or get you down on yours."

Russell stiffened, his gaze locked on the tabletop. *Uh-oh*. Better downshift to a different subject. "So, you got family?" Skip asked.

With a sharp inhale, Russell came up with a smile that looked forced. "Two brothers and two sisters, all older than me."

The bartender interrupted their conversation,

setting their cocktails on the table. After taking a healthy swallow of whiskey, Russell lowered his hand, brushing his knuckles against Skip's fingers. The contact juiced Skip good. He'd have been happy to sit right there all night as long as Russell wanted to hold his hand.

"So you're the baby?"

Russell grimaced. "I suppose."

"Are they all back in Red Wing?" Brothers and sisters were a novelty Skip didn't know much about, so he was sincerely curious.

After another swallow of whiskey, Russell eased back in his seat. "Mostly. Robert's the oldest, and he runs Dad's farm supply company." He spun the whiskey in his glass. "Then there's Dumpling; well, her real name is Regina. She and my other sister Rayanne used to swim with the Aqua Dears, and since I always got dragged to their practices, I learned enough to coach. They're both married and have kids now, though."

On the radio, Chet Baker played "My Funny Valentine," a soft purr in the background. "You're missing one, I think."

Another sigh, this one deep and tinged with sadness. "My brother Rory. He was in the middle, and I guess he always felt bad that he was too young to go fight in Europe." Russell paused and cleared his throat. "When the government started things in Korea, he joined right up." Another pause. "He was killed about four years ago."

Skip was pretty sure he'd stepped into something way more painful than he'd intended. "I'm sorry to hear that."

Russell shrugged, his expression closed. "Can't be helped, but thanks."

"My family's not as big." Did he really want to talk about old news? "Just me and Mom, really. She used to work down here," he said. "She's at Firland now. Got TB."

Russell nodded, a wordless expression of sympathy. Surprised by a sudden burst of emotion, Skip had to look away.

"Yeah." He cleared his throat. "So I work at Boeing, you know? I can't make enough money in this town playing music, and I can't leave until she's better."

"You're so good, though," Russell said, with gratifying enthusiasm. "You're the best horn player I ever heard."

Now it was Skip's turn to blush. "Um…" He rubbed his mouth with an open palm. "Thanks."

Russell reached across the table and laid his hand on Skip's. "And I think it's swell that you're staying here to take care of your mother."

Skip honestly didn't know what to say. Silence filled the space between them.

"Geez," Skip snorted, "if we keep this up, we'll be weepy as a couple of girls." He flipped his hand around to squeeze Russell's fingers before pulling away. "If you want, after this we can go to a club where I can teach you to dance."

"Is that right?" Russell's laugh warmed Skip through and through.

"Yes, sir. The place is down in a basement so no one can see. Gents dance with gents all the time there." Skip gazed up from under his lashes. "And

I'd be happy to dance with a fellow as handsome as you."

Russell turned away, expression so perplexed, Skip had to burst out laughing. A wild spirit took over before he could get himself under control. "So what are you going to do? Go back home and look for Susie's replacement without trying to kiss me?"

Russell went from grinning to furious in a heartbeat. "So what if I am?"

Still caught in the moment, Skip leaned forward. Yeah, he was teasing a tiger, but he couldn't help himself, what with the way Russell's eyes were locked on his mouth. "I don't believe you."

The stare-down lasted several long, hot seconds.

"Fine." Russell downed the rest of his whiskey and banged the glass on the table. "You win. I don't want to go home without kissing you."

"You're in the right place, then. We could go to one of the bathhouses." He talked over Russell's surprised "no." "Or just find a quiet alley. Nobody cares what happens here," he continued. "Skid Road's just a bunch of drunks and fags and musicians, all of us just trying to make enough dough to put food on the table."

"Drunks and fruits and musicians." Russell chuckled.

"You know how us horn players are." Skip fooled with his lower lip, tugging the corner between his teeth, flashing a bit of tongue. Russell followed every move, so much heat in his gaze, it about made Skip steam.

The music changed to something by Billie Holiday, and the bartender strolled over to the end of their table. Raising an eyebrow at Skip, Russell ordered them another round.

They talked, or Skip talked, because even after the alcohol had time to loosen both of them up, Russell still didn't use many words. He smiled, though, and his gaze wrapped over Skip like a comfortable blanket. Past experience taught Skip how to grab a guy and let off steam after a gig. Simple conversation, about his mom and her illness and his dream to move to San Francisco, was new. He'd meant to take Russell's measure, to find out if the big swimming god was a friend of Dorothy too. Instead, he found a man he could be friends with.

The bartender interrupted Skip to ask if they wanted another round.

"What time is it?" Skip guessed it was close to midnight.

"Half past twelve." Russell's eyes were heavy, and Skip's alarm was going to go off at five o'clock. Time to move.

"We can sneak out the back," he said. "It'll be closer to where we parked the car."

He hadn't quite told a lie, but close. They paid for their drinks, and he led Russell toward the back of the narrow room. As soon as they were in the dark hallway, between the tavern and the restroom, Russell backed him up against the wall.

"This is good enough for me."

A firm hand on his chest sent ripples of anticipation through Skip's body. "Me too," he murmured, so close, the warmth of Russell's breath moistened his lips, his internal thermostat driven to the red line by all the teasing and flirting.

"Mmm."

For a screaming instant, he almost stopped, afraid of chasing Russell off. The man had been so skittish, so to make his intentions plain, Skip rocked his hips. In return, Russell's hard heat thrust against his thigh.

"Oh God," Skip said, and Russell met his lips, crushing his head, his shoulders, and his ass into the brick wall.

Russell's body was solid, and he gripped Skip's waist, digging in, nowhere near the touch of a virgin. A groan vibrated up from his belly, and Skip went crazy, both hands grabbing the lapels of the other man's jacket to keep from reaching for his cock. The energy running through them went off like a match thrown in gasoline. It was hard to breathe, hard to stand still. Kissing such a gorgeous man took every ounce of Skip's concentration and hardened a harmless flirtation into bone-deep need.

Russell's lips parted, giving Skip something new to play with. He opened up, sliding his tongue along Russell's lower lip, letting his hands roam over his high cheekbones and close-cropped hair. Their tongues tangled. Whiskers burned his chin. A solid nip to his lower lip almost dropped him to his knees.

They didn't ease off the throttle until someone came looking for the restroom. The man passed them with a murmured, "Careful, boys," and kept moving.

Russell jerked, stiffened, and pulled away. Skip scooted to the side so they stood shoulder to shoulder, their backs to the wall and fingers interlaced, hearts pounding on a backbeat.

"Okay, so dragging you back to the john wasn't my classiest move." Skip flipped his head to clear the flopping bangs out of his face. "That fellow's cool, though. He won't rat on us."

Russell shook their clasped hands. "You don't hear me complaining."

"Yeah, but if Demetrio or the bartender finds us, we'll be out on our cans." Reality kept raining down. "I'd bring you home with me tonight, but I have to work early in the morning."

Russell tipped his head back against the wall and chuckled. "What are we doing here, then?"

"I promised you a drink with a friend." Skip kissed the back of Russell's hand. The kiss turned into a caress, which turned into a tug, and in moments they were in the alley behind the bar. Another couple grappled with each other a dozen feet away, but Skip had a better place in mind anyway. He led Russell midway up the next block, pushed him up a step into a doorway, and knelt in front of him.

"Well." Russell sounded surprised, like he didn't know his way around a quick suck-off, though he was already threading his fingers through Skip's hair.

Skip glanced up once, asking permission, then went to work on the other man's fly. Damp seeped through the knees of Skip's cheap gabardine trousers, but he didn't care. Russell's dick, thick and rosy red, sprang out from his slacks.

He couldn't help himself. He sucked it down,

deep enough that his nose met the forest of curls at the base. Russell made a noise halfway between a groan and a gasp, and his thighs quivered.

Grasping the base with one hand, Skip slid off slowly, teasing, trailing the tip of his tongue around the head.

"Jesus, Mary, and Joseph." Russell's hips hitched, thrust once, and again.

"Mmm." Skip pressed the tip to his lips as he hummed. "Tell me you like this."

Russell's head rocked back, his fingers dragging through Skip's hair. "What?"

"Tell me." He swallowed again, the whole fat length, then slid off, twirling and teasing with his tongue. "You like it." Because Skip liked every bit of it, the scent of sweat and musk, Russell's oddly nervous smile, and the way his whole body trembled. Skip could suck on this cock till the cows came home.

Chuckling at his own pun, he played some more, setting an easy rhythm between his hand and his mouth. "Tell me," he said, then swallowed deep enough to feel the head in the back of his throat. Gave a little cough, and finished the command. "You like it."

Russell was nearly vibrating. "Oh God. Oh yes." He thrust in earnest, banging into Skip, tearing at his hair. "I like it."

Skip got a hand free to cover Russell's mouth and stifle the noise, then reached for his own fly. He'd wanted to kiss Russell, sure, but this was the real McCoy. He sucked hard, his pace going from lazy to rapid to frantic, vaguely aware Russell had a fist mashed against his own lips. *Good boy*.

Russell went rigid and made a noise somewhere deep in his gut. He flooded Skip's mouth with salty, bitter come, and Skip gulped it all down. In the lull that followed, Skip jerked hard on his own shaft, until the white noise of pleasure overrode anything else.

"Hey, are you okay?" Russell smoothed the curls back from Skip's face. "Hey, Lawrence. Speak to me."

Skip nuzzled Russell's thigh. "Call me Lawrence again, and I just might bite it off."

Chuckling, Russell stroked himself, tucking his dick back in his pants. "Now that would be a waste, wouldn't it?"

Skip had to admit, it would. Later, after dropping Russell at the dorm, he had time to wonder how a man who could give himself so fully to some back-alley mambo would ever think about marrying a woman.

## Chapter 8

☾

ON TUESDAY, THE ORGANIZERS PLANNED for the swimmers to take a ferry to Whidbey Island. According to his aunt, it would give them the chance to spread the Seafair cheer along the coast, as if the mere presence of a bunch of tourists from the Midwest would brighten people's day.

The girls had pushed their dining tables to the side so Russell could lead their morning stretches. Midway through, the paper boy interrupted their routine, causing a race to see whose photo made the front page. Afterwards, Russell sacked out in his bunk, hoping they'd leave him alone. He wanted to spend his time reliving those moments in the alley with Skip.

When he wasn't wallowing in shame because of it.

"Are you ready?" His aunt's sharp voice punctured his little fantasy. "The bus leaves in ten minutes."

He rolled over and buried his head under a pillow. "I want to skip this one, Aunt Maude."

"You'll have fun, son." Although she sounded pleasant enough, she gave his doorknob a hard rattle.

The threat of her entrance worked as she intended. He struggled to sit, still tired from a restless night. Still exhausted from his internal battle. "I'll be right there."

The ferry *Evergreen State* was glossy white and smelled like damp metal and diesel exhaust. The school bus loaded with swimmers parked in the empty hull of the boat for the thirty-minute trip. The girls—and Russell—were invited to the viewing deck to admire the forested islands studding the cobalt water.

Along the perimeter of the passenger deck, chocolate-brown banquet seats were perpendicular to big windows. They sat face-to-face and back-to-back, creating spots of pretend privacy. Rows of chrome-framed bench seats ran down the center of the space, and glossy mahogany frames separated the windows. Russell found a seat apart from the girls and their ferocious giggling. There were few passengers besides their group, and the area was quiet except for the growl of the boat's big diesel engines.

A tugboat churned along beside them, headed back toward Seattle. Russell wished he could catch a ride on it, and shut his eyes against the glare of the sun on the water. Skip's question—did he mean to find a replacement for Susie—poked at him like a charley horse he couldn't quite shake off.

A soft "hey" interrupted his introspection. Skip sat at the next bench, his eyes sleepy like he'd just crawled up out of bed.

Utterly flustered, Russell cleared his throat and fought down the sudden surge in his groin. "Shouldn't you be at work?"

"I feel a little under the weather." Skip faked a cough into his fist.

Russell half rose, as much to shake hands as to adjust his slacks and give his cock more room.

"Ryker's shadowing Susie, and I thought you might want a pal too," Skip continued.

Too many emotions pummeled Russell, weighing down his gut. Anger that Susie would have the gall to wave Ryker right in his face. Embarrassment that all the girls would witness his humiliation. Frustration with Skip's heavy-lidded smirk. Shame because of a crazy desire to grab the other man and find a secluded corner.

Back around to anger, this time directed at Skip because he was handy.

"I appreciate the thought, but…" Russell flattened his fingers on his thighs to keep from making a fist. "No."

Skip's grin took on more of a surprised edge. "No?"

"No." Russell's jaw tightened. He didn't want to elaborate, didn't want to explain.

"So, you're going to make me tag along like a third wheel? Because…" Skip scooted over to sit right next to Russell. "I was under the impression you enjoyed my company."

Skip's body heat pulled at him like a magnet. Embarrassed by a shudder of desire, Russell interlocked his fingers and raised his hands high, giving his shoulders a stretch. He needed a good long swim, something hard and fast to get his mind out of the gutter. "I think we have a misunderstanding here." *I'm a lawyer. I can reason this out.*

"I guess we do, because as near as I can tell, people don't notice what they're not looking for. The two of us walking side by side's not going to make anyone think we're a couple of fruits."

Russell swallowed down the urge to slap the smirk off Skip's face. "That's beside the point. I'm not the kind of man you think I am."

"You're lightin' up the tilt sign now, my friend."

"I'm what?" *Don't push your luck, Lawrence.*

"I guess a *college boy* like you never played pinball." Skip shifted his weight, radiating skepticism in the jerky scrape of his hand through his hair.

"Not a college boy anymore."

"Yeah, but you got the jets, so figure it out."

Russell wanted to say something. He opened his mouth, almost forming a word, but closed it again. Skip's full lips distracted him, gave him ideas. Memories. They were fencing over foolishness to avoid the real issue. "I give." He conceded their unspoken game. "What does it mean to light up the tilt sign?"

Skip leaned closer and spoke low, just audible over the rumble of the ferry's engine. "It means you're lying." Then he stood, cool and nonchalant, giving nothing away.

"Lying or not, I can't." Daylight. Aunt Maude. Susie and Annette and all the other swimmers. Russell could come up with a whole list of arguments against palling around with Skip. *People might talk.*

"You were happy enough when I was down on my knees."

"Hush." Russell checked to make sure no one was near. "That was different." Russell turned away so he couldn't see Skip's tongue teasing his lower lip.

"Really?"

"Yes, really."

Skip snorted a laugh. "It's okay to pal around in the dark, in an alley, but not in the light of day." He cracked his knuckles, one hand in the other palm.

"I see."

"I guess I have common sense." Russell glared at Skip until his know-it-all grin faded. He headed for the exit, but Russell glued his gaze to the row of black-and-white life preservers strapped to the wall. Anything so he wouldn't see the breadth of Skip's shoulders and the way his ass moved under his blue jeans. For once, having the last word didn't feel like a victory.

❧

A horn's deep blast marked the end of their journey. Russell kept his head down till well after the bus left the ferry. The day's agenda involved an island tour and a stop at Deception Pass. From the excited twittering coming from the back of the bus, Russell guessed Skip's Buick was following them.

At least Aunt Maude's bulk blocked some of the noise.

"You're quiet today," she said, dragging Russell

into a conversation against his will.

"Mm-hmm." Maybe if he kept his eyes on the road, she'd leave him alone. Russell assumed Susie had made up a story to explain their breakup, somehow making him the bad guy. His belly churned at the thought, thought the memory of his conversation with Skip made him feel worse.

"I've never liked Susie." Aunt Maude's hands rested on her knee, as prim as her clipped words. "I know she meant something to you, but I, for one, am glad you've given her the boot. You're family, and I only want the best for you."

Russell managed a weak "thank you" without meeting his aunt's eyes. They drove past tiny farms, like the ones back home done in miniature, through dense forests dominated by evergreens instead of maples and aspens.

Mountains jutted up raw and craggy along the horizon, a crown of broken teeth surrounding the island. Between the rolling hills and his aunt's placid concern, he felt hemmed in, trapped. He might envy Skip's boldness, but that wouldn't last long in Red Wing. Russell also remembered how the cop recognized "that pervert Skip Johansen." Skip might talk a good game, but Russell suspected things were just as dangerous here as back home for men with certain tastes.

The whole thing made him sick with anger and shame.

A while later, the bus drove down a narrow gravel road and into a parking lot. The group, thirty in all counting the swimmers, coaches, and chaperones, headed down a short dirt path, hemmed in on both sides by enormous evergreens so dense, they blocked out the brilliant sunshine. Then the trees ended, and the gang spilled out into a space about the size of a baseball diamond.

The view opened Russell's heart. They were on the top of a rocky bluff, facing a narrow space between Whidbey Island and the mainland. Above their heads to the left, a high arching bridge connected the two. Forty feet below, waves ran in rags and tatters over craggy rocks designed by the devil.

A man could lose himself in those crashing waves, if ever he reached a point where he couldn't see going on. His gut lurched, muscles clamping down at the mental image of falling, falling. Falling.

He wouldn't let go.

Russell's nature might lead him to groping men in dark places, but he could rise above it, even if the climb looked higher than the mountains edging the horizon. He reached deep, though exhaustion weakened him and he didn't truly know what he was reaching for. Turning away from the temptation in the rolling waves, he vowed to keep his head high.

Back home, they had endless lakes surrounded by forests as old as time. The land was flat, and the Mississippi River rolled along, wide and brown. There were no hills, no mountains, no intoxicating salty air. He clung to the waist-high metal fence, surrendering to the roar of the water and the golden sunshine. Instead of staring out at the endless horizon, he faced his empty future and hoped he'd someday meet a woman who excited him half as much as Skip.

❦

Wednesday morning, Skip jogged across the corner of the giant room, past long rows of airplane bodies waiting patiently like a flock of wingless eagles. The early morning sun made the planes on the east side of the building gleam. Men crawled along the tops, their tool belts loaded, others pushed crates of supplies between rows, and overhead, the fluorescent bulbs flattened out any shadows.

He shot a glance at the giant clock on the wall. Four minutes after. He made it to the office door, pulled his timecard out of the rack, and slammed it home seconds before he'd catch hell. A heavy clunk marked the timeclock's shift to 6:05. Skip stuffed his card back in its slot and was halfway through a pivot to head to put his lunchbox away when a heavy hand landed on his shoulder.

"Mr. Carby wants to see you." The shift foreman jerked his head toward the office.

Jamming with the band till all hours had left him with a muzzy head. Skip blinked, forced a smile and raised his lunchbox. *Couldn't be in too much trouble.* "Soon as I put this away."

"Nope." The foreman's thin face looked somber even when he cracked a smile, and he definitely wasn't smiling now. "You can put it away before you come out on the floor."

His comment let Skip take a breath through a gout of worry. If they expected him out on the floor, he wasn't likely to get fired. He gave the man a quick salute and headed to Mr. Carby's office.

Sliding through the door by the timecard machine, Skip paused in the foyer, where three secretaries had their desks. None of them looked up from their typing. Between the beige linoleum floor and the tan walls, the room reminded him of a bowl of oatmeal. He made sure the collar of his work shirt was straight without acting like the nerdy kid who got called to the principal's office.

The youngest of the three secretaries was his best bet. His smile was two-thirds sincere and one-third flirt, and he rested his rump on the edge of her desk. "Hey, Loretta."

"Well hey, Skip." Her cheeks turned red. She always had perfectly arched brows, painted lips, and sprayed hair. Probably stayed put during sex too, not that he'd ever find out for himself.

"Mr. Carby wants to see me."

"He does?" She lifted the handset of her phone, using the pads of her fingers instead of her long, pink-frosted nails. She dialed with a pencil, and the conversation went on long enough to make Skip's stomach churn. He hadn't done anything wrong, or much wrong, anyway. He'd been late to work a couple of times, maybe, but nothing more serious.

Finally, she dropped the handle back onto the base and gave him a flawless smile. "Go on in."

Still carrying his gray metal lunchbox, Skip knocked on Mr. Carby's door. A muffled response invited him in. He stepped in to the edge of the beige rug. Mr. Carby's desk was oak, and he had pictures on the wall, but it was still a windowless box of oatmeal.

"You wanted to see me?"

"Sit down, Lawrence." Mr. Carby flicked a finger at the straight-backed wooden chair across from his desk. He was a gruff man, a former army major who still kept his hair cut in a precise flat top and who still sat like he had a ramrod for a spine.

Skip dropped into the chair, resting his lunchbox on his lap in case he needed it to protect himself from the firing squad.

"What happened this weekend?" Mr. Carby said, drilling into Skip with his US Army mien.

Skip had no idea what he was talking about. "This weekend?"

"I put out a notice saying everyone was expected to pull at least twelve hours of overtime."

*Damn.* "Sorry, Mr. Carby. I had two shows on Saturday and on Sunday I had to visit my mother."

"Right. Your mother. You know, your foreman told me you're frequently late, and you often come to work looking like you haven't been to bed yet. He also said you took yesterday off to visit your mother." Mr. Carby shuffled the papers on his desk, slashing Skip with razor-sharp glances. "I was so impressed with your devotion, I called Firland. It seems your mother's stable, and they don't have visiting hours on Tuesdays."

The silence in Skip's non-answer echoed between them. He had no defense. He'd lied about needing the day off so he could see Russell.

Russell, who hadn't wanted to hang out with him in the daylight.

Mr. Carby let the silence tick tock with a scowl that had Skip gulping.

"Thank you for not trying to bullshit your way

out of this, son," he finally said. "You've got one more chance, Lawrence." Mr. Carby raised an index finger. "One more."

"Yes, sir."

"Next time I post a notice about overtime, I expect your fanny in here unless it's your mother's funeral."

"Yes, sir."

"Now get out there and stop wasting my time."

Skip cleared the oatmeal office fast enough to break the sound barrier, pretty sure that after his mother's funeral, he wouldn't worry about going back to Boeing ever again. Then he smacked himself for even beginning to think something good could come from his mother's death.

He loved Mom more than any other person on earth. She'd done everything for him, worked at all kinds of trashy jobs so they'd have a decent apartment and he'd be able to take music lessons. Heck, he was probably the reason she had tuberculosis in the first place. She was so wore down when the bugs got her, she couldn't fight it off. Still couldn't, even with the fancy new drugs they pumped into her. Every time he visited, she was thinner, and these days, every time she coughed, she brought up blood.

He moved with sound-barrier speed all the way to the assembly floor, promising himself he'd get his act together. As much as he might hate it, he needed the Boeing job. Getting fired would destroy the rest of his life.

# Chapter 9

〰

AFTER THE SHOW, SKIP HEADED down to the Square, in no mood for any trouble. He parked his car and had gone about half a block when a pair of cops burst out of a quiet little restaurant. He shuffle-stepped to keep from running into the first cop, until his progress was halted by a hand grabbing his shirt.

"Well, look who's here," the officer said. "Skip Johansen. Last time I saw you, you were keeping time with your lawyer. Are you looking to make more work for him?"

Skip jerked out of Officer Murphy's grasp. "Just going to get a drink at the tavern."

"Is that all?" The cop puffed up like a bulldog. His partner leaned against the building with crossed arms and a grin.

"Yep." Using more words would get him in trouble, and Lord knows he could get arrested for hanging out on the wrong block. Lou claimed Murphy secretly carried a torch for Skip, and he abused him rather than admit to it.

"Maybe I should arrest you right now for engaging in lewd behavior."

Skips fought to stay calm, which was tough with irritation taking a shortcut through his belly, heading straight for anger. *Don't give him any ammunition.* "I'm just walking."

Murphy leaned into him, and his partner laughed. "I saw the swing in your hips. Maybe you're trying to attract the wrong kind of attention."

"What are you watching my hips for, Officer?" Skip shifted his weight toward the cop, releasing any remaining grip on his common sense. "Maybe you're the one who should be arrested for lewd behavior."

"You wanna come downtown, Johansen?" His voice dropping to nearly a growl, Officer Murphy gripped Skip's elbow.

His partner pulled Murphy's hand off Skip. "Come on, Murph. We don't have time. We got three more pickups before midnight."

Murphy took a big step and planted his index finger in Skip's chest. "Next time, faggot."

Skip stood still, breathing hard, hands loose at his sides. The cops took off, cocky as a pair of fighters in the ring. Murphy brayed at something his partner said, and Skip waited till they turned onto Washington Street to flip them the bird.

Fear replaced anger, and his hands still shook when he got to the tavern. Instead of ordering his usual beer, he went for a double bourbon on the rocks. It took every drop to block the damned cop from his mind.

"Hey there, big Daddy."

A soft, husky voice spoke right in Skip's ear, followed by a hand on his ass and warm breath nuzzling his neck.

"Lou," Skip said, smirking into his ice cubes. The crowd of men at the tavern sheltered him, even though the recent memories of being here with Russell scraped like sandpaper on his balls.

"Where's your new boyfriend?" Lou asked. He was a slight man, dark haired, with a small mouth and eyes a shade wider than Skip found attractive.

"Boyfriend?"

"Demetrio's telling people you were here with a date, and Bobby Lundquist busted the two of you making out back by the bathroom." Lou slid onto the barstool next to Skip. "Made me jealous, lover boy."

"Aw…" Skip rubbed at a small puddle on the glossy wood bar. After getting lectured by Mr. Carby and blown off by Russell, Lou's outrageous flirting felt good.

"But that's all right, isn't it? I want my Lawrence to be happy." Lou blew a raspberry kiss in Skip's direction. All around, men talked and laughed, and the radio played a Tommy Dorsey tune.

"Slip me the word, cuz. What else did you hear?" There wasn't much to tell, but right then, Skip needed the reminder.

Lou raised a fist. "Number one"—his index finger went up—"I heard he's some kind of Ivy Leaguer."

Skip nodded.

"Number two"—two fingers up—"I heard he was all man, a real bull."

Skip didn't even try to fight the cocky grin.

"And number three"—Lou put up a third finger and made a little moue with his lips—"I heard you looked real gone on him."

Skip ran his hands through his hair. He arched his back. Looked anywhere but at Lou. "Shit." No secrets here. This damned crowd saw and reported every little detail.

He and Russell had had fun. More than fun. Heck, things had been terrific until the morning on the ferry.

"Lawrence Johansen, you are my closest friend." For once, Lou muffled all traces of his nelly guise. "When's the last time you gave the ol' Johnson a workout? Hmm?"

"Shut up, Lou." The part of his anatomy in question stirred, as if acknowledging the attention. "We won't have much chance to work anything out."

"Oh honey, it only takes fifteen minutes." Lou's smile was so innocently naughty, Skip had to smile back.

"Where's he from, anyway?" Lou asked.

"Minnesota…Michigan…some Midwest M state."

"And do you and Mr. Midwest any other dates planned?"

"Says he's not my type." Skip stared at the crowd, avoiding anyone's gaze. He'd played his hand with Russell and been left with a pair of twos.

Lou tapped his lips with his index finger. When he looked up again, he had a swing in his hips, and a sly, feminine smile. "Maybe you need to make him a little jealous. What if Lulu came to see you play?"

"Aw, sweetheart." Skip patted Lou's cheek, affection warring with exasperation. "If you wanna come to a show, let me know and I'll get you a ticket, but I'm not sure it's worth trying to make Russ jealous. He's..." Skip stumbled over a visual of Russell in the soft glow of the stage lights, trim hair, broad shoulders, strong jaw. "No dice."

"Funny, the boys made it sound like he was as snowed as you."

"You know how I am. I fall fast and bounce faster." Skip puffed his lips out with a heavy exhale, avoiding Lou's gaze. "I would bet most of the fellows here tonight go home to their wives or girlfriends and lie about where they've been." The more he thought about it, he knew he was right. "And I understand lying when you have to, but not to me." He crossed his arms, sinking into himself. "Not to my face. Don't tell me you don't like having your dick sucked when I still have the taste in my mouth."

Lou didn't say anything, offering silence as consolation.

Russell had pushed him away easy enough. Time to wake up and smell the coffee. "My boss rattled my cage at work this morning, so I shouldn't run around town all night anyway."

Pulling an old-fashioned pocket watch from his trouser pocket, Lou examined it with wide eyes. "It's midnight, darling."

"You're right." Skip downed the rest of his beer. "I should go."

"Sure." Lou scooted off his stool and planted a wet kiss on Skip's cheek. "You're the most, big Daddy. I hope Mr. Midwest realizes what he's missing."

Skip snorted a wry laugh. "Me too." Whenever possible, Skip avoided men who couldn't look him in the eye, though God help him, he wasn't sure Russell would make it possible.

*

Without Susie's constant chatter in his ear, Russell found he had time to think, and more often than not, his thoughts turned to a certain trumpet player.

Skip had a gift, Russell decided, and it had nothing to do with his horn. He asked the kind of questions Russell didn't like to answer, and he didn't lie. On Friday night, the final notes of a soaring trumpet solo brought a rumble of applause from the sold-out crowd. Well, Russell hadn't caught him in a lie yet, and only a decent man could play with that much heart.

The show went well. Most of the girls had spent the afternoon giving swimming lessons to poor children, so they were tired, but they had perfect timing and crisp cadences. Russell watched from the end of the front row, a spot that gave him a good view of the pool and the band. Not that he watched the musicians.

For once, the air felt like August, muggy and hot enough to force Russell to unbutton his blazer. At the end of the closing number, he followed the line of girls up the path to the locker. There wasn't much chatter. Twelve shows in ten days had taken their toll. The air smelled swampy, and all Russell wanted was a quick shower and a long sleep.

Although if the chance came to talk to Skip, he'd take it. After their last meeting, Russell had been ashamed of himself, though in the early morning hours, a realization had come over him. *Why not?* He'd only be in town for another week. If Skip showed an interest, what was the harm? Russell would have the rest of his life to live the way he should. Missing out on even a minute with Skip would be a damned shame.

A man got only so many chances for love, and though it was wrong, he didn't want to waste this one.

Even Aunt Maude seemed tired. After a perfunctory post-show conference, she retired to the bus, leaving Russell with some time to kill. A few of the girls had come out of the locker, but rather than deal with the crowd of them, he headed down the path along the lake shore. He had a vague idea about walking until he heard Aunt Maude's whistle, then jogged back to catch the bus.

It almost worked, except on the jog back, he came across Ryker, Susie, Annette, and Skip. He tried to keep to the shadows, but his cousin spied him.

"Hey, Russell, we're going dancing. Do you want to come?" Excitement carried Annette's voice half an octave higher than normal.

Russell had no choice but to slow down. "I don't think"—he shot a quick glance from Annette to Susie and back—"that I'm in the mood tonight."

Susie's smile had always seemed so full of light and fun, but now it looked like something painted on a doll. Ryker kept a protective arm around her shoulder, though Russell certainly had no intention of carrying her off.

"I see." Annette shot him an apologetic glance, then smiled up at Skip. Aunt Maude blew her whistle again. "We should go, Susie. We'll see you boys later."

The girls burst into nervous giggles before they'd gone six feet, and Ryker melted away into the darkness. Russell should have headed for the bus, but he couldn't get his feet to move. This was his chance.

"Good show tonight," he said, desperate to bridge the gap between them. Skip chewed on his lower lip, eyes on the water.

"I suppose I owe you an apology." The words burst out, surprising Russell in their sincerity. He'd been reliving their conversation on the ferry all week. If they never said another word to each other, at least he'd know he'd owned up to his mistake.

Skip exhaled, licked his lips, and shoved his hands into his pockets. His trumpet case sat on the damp earth at his feet. "I suppose I shouldn't have surprised you."

"Nah…" Russell scratched at the back of his head. The conversation he wanted to have couldn't happen in public. And he did want to have it. The certainty surprised him as much as the apology had. "I'm only here for a few more days, and, well, I know you're busy tonight, but maybe we could have a drink another time."

Skip watched the water, moonlight highlighting the contours of his face. His beauty broke Russell's heart, while his silence left him floundering.

"I'm buying this time." Russell didn't have a whole lot of money, but he could afford a glass of whiskey for a friend.

With a quick move, Skip picked up his horn. Two steps later, he was close enough for Russell to feel his breath against his cheek. "Thought you weren't a fag like me."

Russell closed his eyes, inhaling the sweet scent of pomade and starch and sweat. "Mostly I feel like a jackass, and I'm…I'm sorry."

"Takes a big man to admit when he's wrong."

There was enough teasing in Skip's voice to make Russell grin. He rocked his hips, once, bumping against the other guy's thigh. "I am a big man."

"Russell?" his aunt called from the bus.

"Just say when." Russell turned up the path. "I owe you."

The heat of Skip's attention stayed with him.

❦

The days passed in a blur of calisthenics and choreography, trips to the laundromat for clean shirts and stilted newspaper photo shoots. Russell spent the shows trying not to make calf's eyes at the orchestra pit, and Skip disappeared every night without taking him up on his offer for a drink. By Sunday, Russell concluded that his attempted apology hadn't worked. The memory of Skip's mouth pressed warm against his lips, the taste of whiskey, and the scratch of whiskers against his chin made the rejection more painful.

Wednesday was closing night. One more show. Their train would leave the next afternoon. Russell marched along the deck like a robot, barking commands at the girls during their warm-up, barely watching their routines. The muggy heat never broke, and before intermission, sweat plastered his button-down shirt to his skin.

Russell had the girls work through some figures. Through grumbles, they began a series of catalinas, cranes, and flamingos. Straightening his tie so the knot sat evenly between the flaps of his collar, he filled his lungs with the boggy, rotten-egg lake smell in an attempt to wash away the puddle of melancholy sloshing around in his gut.

Susie broke ranks, pulling up to the side of the pool to work out a cramp. Under other circumstances, he'd give her a quick scold and send her back to the water. Tonight he ignored her, telling himself she was the cause of his unhappiness.

*Who am I kidding?* His relief at being done with Susie was almost pathetic. Heat built in his groin, a slow swelling, a pressure so sweet, it caused pain. He wanted Skip. Now. He didn't want to go off into some mythical future without touching him. Tonight. The lanky musician didn't fight his nature, and Russell needed another taste of his life.

He stuffed his hands in his trouser pockets to hide his clenched fists. He could wish and want and hope all night long, but if he wasn't willing to do anything about it, he'd end up alone.

Before the show started, the director stood at the edge of the stage and gave the performers a pep talk. He assured the dancers the crew would do their best to keep the stage dry if it rained, and complimented the swimmers on a fine performance the night before. Russell's gaze drifted over to the band, right about the time Skip looked in his direction, and the director might have been a dog barking down the block

Russell smiled, as broad and inviting as possible. Skip didn't return his smile, but he didn't turn away either. His expression might have softened, or maybe the distance and the misting rain blurred his features the way fog turned oak trees into green-gray smudges.

The moment passed.

Skip lifted his horn and laughed in response to something Russell couldn't hear. Aunt Maude waved from stage left, demanding Russell's attention, reminding him of what was possible.

And what was not possible.

The girls made it through the Aqua Dixie minstrel number without any problems. Their moves were sharp, elegant, and their smiles brilliant. Russell allowed himself to relax, even laughed at the MC's tired jokes.

Then the conductor counted off "In the Mood."

Skip rose above the band to play his solo, and desire crystalized in Russell's soul, brittle enough to cut deep if it shattered.

But he felt more than desire, more than the simple physical urge a man could handle on his own. He wanted to know Skip, to share in the warmth of his optimism. Russell shut his eyes, indulging in the trumpet's bell-like tone. A kiss meant something. Both the giver and the receiver had to lower their guard, leave themselves open. They'd done a lot more than just kiss, but still, he couldn't get on the train to Red Wing without talking to Skip one last time.

They still had things to say to one another.

Tonight after the show, he'd give Aunt Maude the slip and wait in the parking lot. He and Skip would have their chance, and if things backfired, at least he'd know he'd given it his best shot.

Right before the grand finale, the swimmers posed along the edge of the deck, a row of sherbet-colored dolls, their left legs extended, toes pointed, arms held gracefully overhead. One by one, each turned her arabesque into a dive and hit the water right in time with the band, so steady, Russell kept track with a nod of his head. Three from the end, Phyllis slipped, stumbled, hit the water at an odd angle. The misfire jerked his attention in her direction and he was moving from his spot on the deck before her bubbles rose to the surface.

He rounded the deck at a near run, acting from such a basic level, it was almost instinct. The rest of the girls side-stroked toward the stage, facing over their left shoulder for four-beat strokes, then flipping to their right. Phyllis was still underwater, a vague shadow wrestling with an invisible adversary. Russell tossed his blazer onto the deck and kicked out of his shoes, sliding down into the water with a minimum of splash, doing his best not to attract the audience's attention.

The routine went on, the band played, and Russell filled his lungs and dove. Silence. Cold. One strong pull of his arms brought him close to her. Phyllis grabbed his hand hard, before he was ready, her nails digging into his flesh. He almost gasped, recovered, took hold of her arm, and kicked them both to the surface.

They broke through the water with a crash of cymbals and a huge roar from the crowd. Phyllis coughed hard between gulps of air. Russell got his arm around her chest and dragged her over to the deck. She held on to the ledge with one hand, and he launched himself out of the water, planted his feet, and hoisted her out. She made it onto her hands and knees.

"I breathed water"—a racking cough made her chest heave—"couldn't find up."

Russell quickly surveyed the area. Only a few people were watching them. Most everyone's attention was on the divers careening off the platforms, tripping over their floppy clown feet and splashing the crowd.

A man tapped Russell on the shoulder. "I'm a doctor. Let me help you get her off to the side."

Russell was grateful for the help. They needed to get Phyllis someplace where she wasn't on stage.

The man barely came to Russell's shoulder and was probably the same age as his father. Phyllis was doubled over coughing, and Russell knelt to help her up, terrified by her struggle to breathe. The doctor took hold of her arm, and together they got her standing. Russell looped her arm over his shoulders, lifted her under her knees, and carried her off the deck toward the lockers.

Once they were behind the stage, the noise from the show diminished. Phyllis's coughing slacked off too, though she still clutched at Russell. Her chest heaved, and shivers racked her body. After a quick conversation, the doctor stayed with Phyllis while Russell went into the locker to get her belongings.

She was still coughing when Russell returned. "We should get her to a hospital," the doctor said. "Wait here, and I'll go get my car."

He jogged off, and Russell wrapped Phyllis in a towel. Her coughing paused long enough for her to gasp words out. "Can't catch my breath."

With the flat of his palm, Russell made circles on her back. He didn't know her very well, but her ribs' frantic heaving frightened him. "You must have hit the water wrong."

"Yeah." She gave in to another burst of coughing.

Aunt Maude strode up, heels hitting the pavement so hard, they could have shot sparks. "What happened?"

Between bursts of coughing, Russell and Phyllis tried to explain. By the time they were done, the doctor was back with his automobile.

"We're going to Harborview County Hospital." He spoke with such authority, Aunt Maude shut up.

"I'll go with her, Aunt," Russell said. "You take the team back to the dorm."

Her look of fear flayed him. "Take care of her."

"We will." The doctor patted his aunt's shoulder, a gesture that would have earned anyone else a quick swat.

Aunt Maude heaved a sigh. "Okay. I'll get someone to drive me over there once all the girls are in bed."

"Sure," Russell said. His aunt might have been a prickly pear, but she was committed to her girls. "She'll be okay."

Russell and Phyllis climbed into the doctor's car, a new white Chrysler with lots of chrome. They pulled out of the parking lot, and Russell's belly clenched, his breath caught tight in his chest. The emergency had overruled his plans. He'd probably never see Skip again. Never have the chance to show him how he felt. He plunged into a cold sadness he couldn't put aside despite Phyllis's distress.

# Chapter 10

❧

FOR THE LAST TIME, SKIP held down the spit valve and blew through his horn, sending a spray of liquid onto the floor of the pit. For the last time, he unscrewed the mouthpiece and laid his trumpet in its case. For the last time, he said good night to the show's director.

The 1955 Aqua Follies had ended.

Most of the stage lights had been shut off, and the empty stands echoed with stragglers' laughter. A few musicians were still packing up, and after his usual whining, Ryker had hauled his first load of gear to his car.

Skip snapped the buckles on his trumpet case and climbed out of the pit. Earlier, he'd done his best to ignore the way Russell's trim charcoal suit emphasized his broad shoulders and long legs. Skip owned one suit, black gabardine, cut too wide. He wore it for gigs and would wear it to his funeral, and he huffed with jealous appreciation at the way Russell managed to look both athletic and smooth.

He hurried down the ramp to shore. Didn't matter how good Russell looked. No point in bellyaching over what he couldn't have.

Halfway to the parking lot, Skip bumped into Ryker.

"Man, your horn wailed tonight." Ryker extended his hand to shake.

"And you were the boss on the beat." Skip switched his horn case to his left hand and offered Ryker his right. "Do you need a ride home?"

A woman's giggle from the direction of the lockers made Ryker twitch. "Nah, I've got my father's big V8."

"The Thunderbird?"

"Yes, sir, Daddy-O. I've got things to do tonight."

"Where you going?"

"Gonna kill some time at a jam, then, when everyone's asleep, I'm snatching Susie and we're heading for California."

Skip almost dropped his horn. "California?" What the heck? California was his dream, where he could earn a living playing music. Just hearing the word prompted visions of cable cars and Chinese food and jam-packed jazz clubs.

*Damn.* The irony burned in his gut like a shot of cheap booze. Ryker kept talking, but Skip barely listened.

"Well, to start with, we're going to my cousin's in Tacoma." Ryker reached for his pack of smokes, his shiny chrome lighter glinting. "Did you catch the sideshow tonight?" Hot red flame threw his face into shadow. "One of the swimmers almost drowned, I guess."

A second surprise jerked Skip out of the muddle of his own thoughts. "What?"

"Yeah, Susie says they all want to go to the hospital to see her, but the old battle-ax won't let them." Ryker paused, flicked his lighter, and inhaled.

Russell would be upset too, though Skip kicked himself for worrying about him.

Ryker exhaled a cloud of smoke and carried on, oblivious. "Russell took the girl, Phyllis, I think is her name, to Harborview County."

"Damn."

"Susie figures Mrs. Ogilvie will be busy at the hospital, so this is our chance to bug out." He took another drag. "Besides, they take the train tomorrow, and I'm not letting this one go."

*I'm not letting this one go.* Skip didn't ever expect to say those words. As much as he liked a little backseat bingo, he wasn't about to risk his heart for someone who'd soon be on a train out of town.

Maybe they'd both acted like jackasses on the ferry, but Russell's apology made it worse. In one flirty, honest gesture, Russell had turned into someone Skip could care about. *No way.* He'd spend every night down at the baths before he'd let himself fall in love.

Ryker bumped him with an elbow. "I'll see you later. Gotta grab the rest of my kit then head over to the 443."

Normally, Skip would have been eager to jam at the Negro Musician's Union, the 443. Normally, he would have offered to help haul drums to Ryker's car. This night wasn't normal, and his temper was foul enough he'd likely end up in a fight.

Besides, one of the perks of being a horn player was only having a single case to drag around. Skip sauntered across the parking lot, ignoring the jagged lights from the school bus and the jabbing disappointment from knowing Russell wasn't there.

(

The next morning dawned clear and perfect. Not trouble-free—Russell had had too little sleep and too much on his mind for that—but clear and comfortably warm. The crystalline blue sky drew him outside to the small lawn in front of the dorm, where the light swirling breeze carried the scent of the ocean.

Something about Seattle enticed him, drew him in. Home had its beauties, but there was a sameness to the flat stretches of green. Seattle was a young city, still grappling with the surrounding mountains, oceans, and lakes. Everywhere he turned, he was distracted by the rugged natural beauty.

He could live here, if things were different. If he wasn't afraid of breaking his mother's heart.

Russell's feet were restless, but rather than give in to the yen for a long run, he sought out his aunt. The group would be traveling today, and he needed to make sure he understood his role in her plan.

He found her in the dorm cafeteria, a long room that smelled of burnt coffee and toast. Annette was with her, sitting with her back to Russell at the far end of one of the dining tables. Aunt Maude had her hand on Annette's shoulder, her face so grim, it could have been carved from marble. Coming closer, he heard the sobbing.

Annette's shoulders were hunched and her hands covered her face. Her hair was still in curlers, covered with a coral chiffon scarf. Aunt Maude's eyes were ringed dark, but she had her lipstick on and her flowered shift was crisp. She murmured to Annette, though Russell couldn't tell if they were words of comfort, or something else.

"Aunt Maude?" He kept a chair or two between himself and the women and spoke softly, doing his best not to intrude.

"Good morning, Russell." His aunt waved him into a chair. "Better you hear this now rather than later."

He scooted back a chair and sat, resting his forearm on the table. "What?"

"She left." Annette hiccupped into her hands. "Susie took off with that Ryker guy, and says she's not coming back."

*Not coming...?* Russell's head jerked as if her voice had been an actual slap in the face. His mind puzzled out the words, trying to make them fit in a rational sequence. He and Susie had once been happy. Hadn't they? Before she left? Maybe she'd just been using him. Except he really wasn't good for much, so using him would have been a waste of her time. Of course, maybe she figured that out, and that was why she left.

"Oh Russell," Annette wailed. "I'm so so-o-o-rry."

Aunt Maude settled heavily into the chair across from Annette. "Hush now, honey. Your eyes will stay puffy all day." When Annette kept up the noise, Aunt Maude rapped sharply on the table.

"That's enough."

Annette hopped in her seat, but she quieted down.

"The problem is…" Aunt Maude paused to dump some creamer in her coffee. She tasted it, made a bitter face, and kept talking. "Phyllis will be staying in the hospital for the next few days, and her parents won't be able to fly out here right away. I'm going to need you to stay behind, Russell, to be with her until they get here."

Flustered, Russell rose to get himself a cup of coffee. It was easier to move than to sort through all the ideas the last few minutes had presented him with. "Okay."

"I would like you to do something else, Russell, though I know this will be difficult for you."

He glanced warily at her over the top of the brown pottery mug. "Yes?"

She looked so profoundly unhappy, he knew what she was going to say before the words left her mouth. "I would like you to find Susie and talk her into coming with you to Detroit."

*Why not just ask me to empty Lake Erie with a teaspoon?* "Aunt Maude…"

"I know, but her parents will be distraught. She held you in some regard, so maybe she'll listen to what you tell her." Maude's posture firmed, as if the conviction with which she spoke strengthened her backbone. "She'll be a little soiled, but if we get her home quickly, her parents will still be able to marry her off to someone."

His aunt's considering tone of voice made Russell angry. The Susie he knew was flighty, sometimes silly, but she rarely did things without thinking about the consequences. But then he'd thought she was going to marry him.

Just went to prove how little he knew about women anyway.

"Mother." Annette distracted him with a full-throated wail. "I was supposed to be her maid of honor."

"Well, now you'll have to find a different drama to star in," Aunt Maude said acerbically.

"*Mo-ther.*" His cousin's cry drove Russell to his feet.

"Is there anything else, Aunt Maude?" Russell used the calmest tone of voice he could muster, though after the bombshell his aunt dropped, it wasn't easy.

"Yes, Russell." Exhaustion riddled his aunt's voice. "This afternoon when I'm at the train station, I'll change your ticket and Susie's so you can take the train directly to Detroit for the next run of shows. We're scheduled to have four days at home, so if you and Susie take the train next Wednesday, we should all arrive in Detroit on the same day."

Desire shimmered in Russell's belly. Five, maybe six more days in Seattle. He just needed to keep Phyllis company, find Susie, and avoid Skip. Or find Skip and avoid Susie. Russell felt punch-drunk. "I think I'm going to change into shorts and sneakers and go jogging." He tugged on his khaki pants. "And then I'll figure out how to take the public bus to the hospital."

Aunt Maude rose too. "You'll need to clear out of here by today. Do you have money for a hotel?"

Russell pulled out his wallet. "About twenty dollars."

"Well, here." Aunt Maude handed him another twenty. "That's for a hotel room and some food." Her lips thinned, and she blinked once. "I'm sorry, but I don't have any more."

She stuffed the bill into his hand, and he took it because he had the strong impression his Aunt Maude would burst into tears if he didn't. If Aunt Maude cried, the world truly was going to hell. Russell stuffed the cash in his wallet and forced a smile. "I'll just take a short run, then pack up my stuff."

"We won't be leaving here till noon," she said.

The grim determination in the tilt of her chin reminded him of his mother, her sister. "I won't let you down."

In a way, he spoke to both of them.

# Chapter 11

(6

RUSSELL SPENT THE AFTERNOON IN the lobby of the Harborview County Hospital, where the recalcitrant sun dragged squares of gold across the linoleum floor. Despite—or maybe because of—his aunt's sympathetic attitude, he reckoned the whole team was laughing at him.

Wondering if her request was really a way for him to save face.

After one more check on Phyllis, he went to the restroom and splashed cold water on his face. Blinking bleary-eyed in the old, crazed mirror, he smacked himself for making such a mess of things. He'd find Susie, and not just because his aunt told him to. He'd find her and convince her to talk to her parents. He'd find her because taking care of his friends was the sort of thing a man did. He'd find her because he didn't trust Ryker, no matter what Skip said.

That wasn't good enough.

He left Phyllis napping and checked himself into a hotel. The place didn't look like much, and the smell of old socks and mold almost scared him off, but the hospital receptionist had said it was the cheapest place around.

The Seattle weather had finally warmed up, so Russell left his blazer and tie in the hotel room closet. Dressed in a pink-striped sport shirt and khaki slacks, he strode down the hotel's hall, barely lit by faux Roman wall sconces between each doorway. Waiting for the narrow Otis elevator, he rehearsed his reasons for tracking Skip down.

Pretty simple, really. Skip was his only connection to Ryker, and he figured Demetrio at the bar was his best connection to Skip.

He maintained his confident act all the way to the street, when he realized he wasn't sure where to go. They'd been down near the waterfront, but, surrounded by cars and ten-story buildings, the ocean was hard to find. The hulking carcass of Harborview County Hospital, however, waited just down the block.

Back in the hospital lobby, the daytime receptionist had gone home, her rhinestone brooch and cat-eye glasses replaced by a dumpy older man with four long clumps of hair spread across his glossy pate. "What can I do for you, young man?"

Smoke from his cigarette singed Russell's nose. "If you could direct me to that big totem pole, that'd be swell."

"You're not from around here." The old guy stuck his cigarette in the corner of his mouth. "Lemme send you someplace a little nicer."

"No, I'm…ah…" Russell scrambled for an explanation. "A friend of mine…my cousin, really… works near there in a tavern. I have to tell him about, ah, his mother."

The guy shifted the cigarette from one side of his mouth to the other, as if the motion would help him evaluate the truth in Russell's excuse. "If you say so. Go out to Yesler Way and head downhill. You'll find it." He pointed off to his right. "You be careful, son. You look sturdy enough, but it's a rough neighborhood."

"Thank you," Russell said, responding by force of habit. He headed through the modern lobby, making a right at the street. Yesler Way cut down a hill overlooking the waterfront, with a view of half the world.

"This city," Russell murmured, "is the most amazing place on earth."

The road leveled off after about a mile, landing Russell right under the totem pole. He retraced the steps they'd taken from Pioneer Place to the tavern, past the neon Seattle Hotel sign and the wrought-iron awning. Every step twisted the tension running up the back of his neck. He remembered the man selling peanuts and the coffeehouse for women. He remembered the stuffy little tavern where he'd been able to breathe.

Would Skip remember? Would he help?

The neighborhood hadn't seemed too bad when he'd been here with Skip. Now, though, it looked as rough as the man at Harborview County had promised. On Russell's right there were slices of deep-ocean emptiness between buildings, and the air was heavy with the stink of salty fish. Across from him, a man sat on the sidewalk, his knees bent, head down, and the neck of a bottle protruding from a paper bag in his hand.

Russell jogged across the street, stepping wide around the man with the bottle. Buildings blocked what was left of the day's sun, and the shadows between them made the skin between his shoulder blades crawl.

A woman stepped out from an unlit doorway, and Russell's heart bucked into his throat.

"Hey there, wanna date?" Her lipstick was sloppy, and a cigarette dangled between her fingers.

"No, I'm sorry. I'm looking for a friend." Russell kept moving.

"I can be your friend," she called after him.

"Sure," he whispered.

He passed a coffee shop, and sure enough, only women sat at the little round tables. Another block down, he recognized the swarthy man who had greeted Skip by calling him Lawrence. Russell straightened to his full height under the man's stern gaze.

"Hello." He put on his company smile and extended his hand to shake. The man in the doorway didn't take it immediately.

"You wouldn't remember me." Russell felt dumb. "I'm Russell. I was here the other night with Skip Johansen."

"Demetrio." The swarthy man thawed out enough to shake Russell's hand. His fingers were soft and warm, and his grip slid away in an extended caress.

"Do you know Skip? You called him Lawrence."

"You were his date." The man crossed his arms, and the look he fixed on Russell was either cross or mocking or both.

"I need to find him. It's important."

The man chuckled, his lower lip thrusting out to lead the rest of his mouth in a smile. "It always is with you youngsters."

"Is he here?"

"Haven't seen him yet. He and Lou were here pretty late last night." Demetrio must have noticed Russell's disappointment. "I tell you what." He gave Russell's shoulder a heavy-handed rub. "If he comes in tonight, I'll tell him you stopped by." With another sympathy pat, the man waved Russell in. "Grab a seat by the bar. He might have a gig tonight and be in later."

Russell eased out of the man's enthusiastic grip. Lunch had been a dry ham sandwich in the hospital cafeteria, which wouldn't absorb a whole lot of alcohol, but a glass of whiskey and a bowl of pretzels could probably help him figure out what to do next.

"Good idea."

Russell settled himself at a booth and signaled the bartender. In short order he had his whiskey and his pretzels, but they didn't bring him any closer to figuring out what to do. He'd nearly finished his first shot when there was a commotion at the door. Three women walked in, screeching with laughter and greeting some of the men on their way down the bar.

They wore dresses and heels, lipstick and pearls, but their calves were too muscular, and the stocky one gripped her purse with hairy man hands.

The group's apparent leader, a petite brunette

in a lavender suit and white heels, swung down the narrow center aisle and stopped at Russell's booth. Russell froze under her scrutiny, clutching his empty cocktail glass.

She pursed her lips as if fighting a smile, then surrendered with a broad smirk. "The stories were right. You are all man, aren't you, my dear?" She slipped into the booth across from him.

"Excuse me?"

"I am Lulu, and my ex-boyfriend is so gone on you, he can't find his ass with both hands."

The bottom dropped out of Russell's gut. "What?"

The other two women leaned over his table, cooing and giggling. One, her brassy red hair rolled and pinned in a sleek chignon, snatched a handful of pretzels and popped them one at a time between her blood-red lips.

"Oh sweetie, don't look so terrified." Lulu reached over and rested her gloved hand on Russell's.

Using his best manners, Russell turned Lulu's attempt to fondle him into a handshake. "I'm Russell."

Lulu wouldn't let go, her grip tightening hard enough to rub his knuckles together. "I've heard all about you, and now I want to know what you did to hurt my friend." Her voice was more strident than Ethel Merman on a high note.

Russell exhaled hard, rubbing his mouth with his free hand. He needed a shave, he needed Lulu to let go of his hand, and he needed to talk to Skip. "I don't know your friend. I'm sorry."

"Oh yes you do." Lulu's voice rose to a squeal, a blend of triumph and humor and maybe compassion. "You came here looking for him tonight." She squeezed his hand again, hard. "Skip Johansen's my very best friend, and before I tell you how to find him, I want to know what you did."

Skip's name choked Russell like a noose around his neck, so tight he couldn't comprehend the rest of her message. He jerked his hand away from her and half rose in his seat.

The redhead snickered through her pretzels, and the chunky one guffawed, her beefy hands clutching her pearls. Russell lowered himself in the seat and closed his mouth, embarrassed to have been caught with it hanging open.

"You've really got him scared now, Lulu," the beefy one said. Her voice was deeper than it should have been, but her smile was kind.

"This one's a farm boy." Lulu took hold of his hand again. "But Skippy likes him." She popped open the clasp on her shiny gold clutch purse and drew out a pen and a little notepad. Her perfume distracted Russell, blending roses with the scent of incense from a Catholic church.

"Main 2471." She slid the note across the table, keeping her fingers on a corner. "Skip's telephone number."

With two fingers, Russell tried to slide the paper to his side of the table, but she didn't let go.

"If you're not nice to him," her voice dropped, getting meaner, "I will be very unhappy." She lifted her fingers, splaying them out with a bubbling laugh and washing away most of the anger.

Russell tucked the note in the inner pocket of his jacket. "Thank you."

"Now the girls and I have to go." Lulu scooted out of the booth. "We've got a show tonight at the Garden. Come by later if you want to have some fun."

"We can be lots of fun." The redhead blew him a kiss.

Laughter carried the three of them out to the street. In a moment of quiet, the bartender brought Russell a second whiskey. Russell relaxed into the cushioned booth, gazing at the amber liquid, allowing the day to settle.

Lulu's visit was the sweet finishing touch to the day's difficulties. First Phyllis, then Susie, then Aunt Maude. He debated whether he'd reached his limit and should catch a cab back to the hotel.

Well, he couldn't afford to be taking cabs anywhere. Instead, he reached in his pocket for a nickel, trying to remember if he'd seen a telephone booth out on the street.

℃

The phone in Skip's apartment rang twice in quick succession. His ring. Not the neighbor's long single ring or the long-short from down the hall. His ring on the party line.

*What the heck does Lou want now?*

He rolled off the bed, catching himself right before he landed on the floor, and picked up the receiver.

"Skip? It's Russell."

The air left Skip's lungs as if he'd been shot with

a gun. He didn't want to talk to Russell. He wanted to forget. Dragging his fingers through his hair, he marshalled some words of his own.

Behind the silence on Russell's end, a car's horn honked. Women's voices. Street noise. *He isn't on a train.* "What are you even doing? Where are you?"

"By the tavern, on Second Avenue and, ah…" The background noise got muffled, as if Russell had pressed the receiver against his chest. "Washington, I think."

"Well, what's your story, morning glory?" Skip dropped into the one comfortable chair, hunched over, propping his elbows on his thighs. Whatever the story was, he had a feeling he wouldn't like it.

Russell took so long to respond, Skip tracked most of a conversation happening out on the street, something about a liquor store with beer on sale. When he couldn't wait any longer, he tried again. "Russ?"

"I'm sorry. I have a favor to ask." A rapping noise interrupted him. "Just a minute," Russell said, though Skip couldn't tell who he was talking to. Again the sound from the phone was muffled, with only broken phrases making it to Skip's end.

"Sorry," Russell said after a moment.

"You keep saying that."

"What?" Stress zinged over the line.

"Sorry."

"I'm so… Wait." Russell chuckled, and Skip finally took a breath. His whole body buzzed with tension. It was only about six o'clock, plenty early enough for…all kinds of things.

"I was wondering if, well, could you meet me

down here for a drink? Please?" Russell sounded cool, the way he'd sounded when he told off Officer Murphy after the jam session.

*Must be nervous.* Skip's resistance softened, but drinks at the bar would surely end up further than he wanted to go. "I'll pick you up, and we'll go get a burger somewhere." He'd just been lying around feeling sorry for himself, anyway.

"I would offer to pick you up, but—"

"You left your rocket at home."

The rapping sound started again. "There's a guy who might die if I don't give him the phone booth." Russell sounded irritated, and Skip had to smile imagining Mr. Midwest's glare.

"Be careful. He might want to do perverted things to you."

The silence between them got real heavy real quick. "But I don't want to do perverted things with him."

The weight on the final word left Skip with little doubt about his meaning. He didn't know why Russell was still around, but real quick decided not to look a gift horse in the muzzle. "Walk out of the Square." Skip wasn't one bit ashamed of the roughness in his voice. "Toward the totem pole. I'll be down there in ten minutes."

"I'll be waiting."

# Chapter 12

## ✿

THE CAR. BLACK AND BULKY. Cracked vinyl seats sucked Russell in. Skip's profile caught light and shadow from oncoming traffic, a half grin softening the lines. He drove with one hand on the wheel, the other arm cocked so his elbow rested on the open window. Pioneer Square was behind them, and after about two blocks, Russell lost any sense of landmarks and location. They drove along quiet streets, past office buildings and shops, stiffness working its way down Russell's spine and tying his shoulders in knots.

Skip pulled to a stop at a red light, his raised brow catching Russell's eye. "So you're still in town."

"Where are we headed?" Russell spoke over top of Skip's comment, too nervous to stop himself. The last time those lips had been so close, they'd been wrapped around his cock.

"There's a place over in Wallingford." From the heat in his voice, Skip might have been thinking the same thing. "I'll buy you a burger, but only if you tell me what's going on."

"What?"

"Dick's Drive-Inn. You know, hamburgers. Don't they have those in Montana?"

Russell snorted. "It's Minnesota."

"Isn't that the same place? I flunked geography." Skip's grin gleamed through the semidarkness, halfway between a promise and a dare.

Russell adjusted his jacket, afraid to look in Skip's direction. That hint of flirtation had sidetracked his hunger and bolstered his resolve to keep his mind on business. "You asked why I'm still here."

"I am a little curious." Skip eased the car to a stop and stretched out his arm, draping it over the back of the seat, fingertips resting lightly on Russell's shoulder. "Didn't expect to see you again."

Russell took a deep breath, made a fist with his right hand, and pressed it against his left palm. One knuckle gave a loud pop. Part of him wanted to stop, to talk, to clear the air before driving any further down this path to the unknown.

The rest of him wanted Skip alone in a dark room with the door locked.

Flexing his fingers, he forced that thought away. "This is awkward, you see, because it has to do with Susie." He'd had all day to rehearse his lines, but he still got snarled up. "She…" He squinted into the setting sun. "She ran off with Ryker, and my aunt asked me to find her and bring her back to Red Wing."

The light ahead of them turned green, but the car didn't move. Skip was laughing too hard to drive. "That is the *most*," he managed to choke out.

"Just drive," Russell grumbled. The car behind them honked their horn.

"All right. Keep your pants on." Still chuckling, Skip drove along. They'd gone several blocks when he shot Russell a brash grin. "Ain't that a gas? And here I thought you stuck around for my good looks."

*Any way I slice it, I'll end up in trouble.* "Maybe." He let the word slide, flirting right back, then kicking himself for giving Skip encouragement. This was about Susie, not the sweaty heated hijinks two men could get up to. If he were a judge, he'd throw down the gavel. "Will you help me find her?"

They pulled up to another stoplight, and Skip leaned over to his side of the seat. "I will, but it might cost you."

Russell couldn't sidestep a challenge like that, though in a car with the windows open in the daylight, the best he could do was to keep from backing away. "Depending on what you come up with, we'll see."

Skip flipped the turn signal, heading into the parking lot of a glossy orange, white, and neon drive-in. "I guess we will see."

The place smelled like grease and salt, and the fries were the best Russell had ever tasted. He insisted on buying Skip's dinner, though it cut into his forty dollars, and he leaned back against the door, savoring the last few bites.

"So what are you going to do?" Skip asked. "Bribe Susie into coming home with that ring you've been carrying around in your pocket?"

Russell shot up in the seat. *How did he know?*

"No, I—"

"Or are you just going to find some other girl to give it to, even though we…" Skip flicked a finger between the two of them.

Russell bit down hard on a stream of obscenities. Provoking the driver wouldn't get him very far. His nostrils flared as he inhaled. "It's not like"—he flicked his finger back and forth—"we could get married."

"Is that the goal, then? Getting married?"

"Don't you want to?" The car's cracked upholstery dug into his thighs.

Skip teased his lower lip with his teeth. "Not if it means I can't…" Again he flicked his finger.

Russell got the message. "But this"—he waved his hand back and forth—"is against the law."

Skip gave him a puzzled frown. "So don't tell anyone."

Someone in another car turned on their radio, and Jerry Lee Lewis pounded through their open windows. "Demetrio and his friend Gabe have lived together for ten years," Skip continued. "I'm sure they keep two bedrooms and mess up both beds, but—"

"That's the thing, though," Russell said. "Someone could break into their house and steal their good silver, and if they called the cops, they'd be the ones arrested."

"Maybe." Skip balled up his burger wrapper and tossed it into the bag. "But I think I'd rather take that chance than marry some girl."

"Susie wasn't just *some girl*." Something crumbled in Russell's hands. The burger. He stuffed the last bite in his mouth to keep from saying anything he'd regret.

"That's right. I forgot. You were in love with her."

*Love* sounded like a dirty word. Russell chewed and swallowed, too angry to respond.

Skip ran his fingers along the steering wheel like he was playing scales. "I mean, you were in love with her, right?"

"I care about her a great deal." Arms crossed, Russell dared Skip to challenge him.

With a cocky smirk, Skip mouthed his words back to him...*a great deal.*

"I did." Frustrated, Russell threw up his hands. "I do."

Skip shook his head. "I thought getting married meant falling in love, like you'd be ready to pick up and die for a person." Another thoughtful pause. "Or die without them."

The radio in the car next to them switched from Jerry Lee to Chuck Berry. Russell didn't want to carry on a conversation about love with a man. "Will you help me find her?"

Skip took a long swallow from his soda pop. "I'll make a couple phone calls."

*Better than nothing.* "Thank you."

☾

"So what now?" Skip headed the car south on Highway 99. This night wasn't going the way he thought it would. Bringing up Demetrio and Gabe had started him thinking about the couples he knew, the ones who were happy. That had started him digging at Russell. *Fair?* Didn't matter. They'd be out of each other's hair soon enough.

"My hotel's over by Harborview County."

*Moody bastard.* "I'll drop you off and get your room number so I can leave you a message if I hear from Ryker."

Russell grimaced. "Sure. Thanks."

A devil took hold of Skip's soul. "Unless you want me to come up for a while."

"Um…" Russell faced away, as if the Twin Teepees Diner held some incredible fascination. "Yeah."

"Yeah what?" He could hear Lou shrieking in his head. *Leave it alone, Skippy.*

Russell's smile tried to cover…what? Shame? Pain? "Yes, Skip. I want you to come up to my room."

Skip didn't know whether to be relieved or dismayed.

They drove in silence until Skip turned the car radio on to fill in the gaps. Dean Martin sang something mellow, turning up the heat. Skip was caught on a high wire, and he was going to hate the fall. His body wanted, though, and if his feelings went deeper than that, he could ignore them.

Russell directed him to a small, run-down building a block from the hospital. Skip parked across the street and did his best not to make a face on the way into the lobby. "I hope this place is cheap."

"Cheap enough."

He followed Russell up a narrow staircase to the second floor. Two doors down the hall, Russell stopped. "It's not much," he said.

Skip scuffed the ratty carpet with his toe. "You had to pick the only lousy place in this neighborhood."

"The receptionist said it was cheap." A pair of Chinamen came out of a room down the hall. "Evening," Skip said, giving them a nod. Russell didn't manage that much. "So it's Thursday now."

Russell got the door unlocked and stepped aside to let Skip in.

"And your train tickets are for Wednesday, right?" Skip continued, taking in the shabby room, with the locked suitcase sitting on a twin bed.

"Yes." Russell closed the door.

For a heartbeat, Skip teetered on the edge of indecision. Only a fool would willingly get involved with something so likely to end in pain. *But Wednesday will be here soon.* "Get your bag. You can come stay with me."

"Why? This place is…" Their gazes caught and held. Russell broke away first, his cheeks scarlet. "I know, but I couldn't afford more."

Skip understood. He spent most of his life balanced on the edge. There were nicer hotels just one or two blocks away, but they were a lot more expensive. "Save your money. You don't know how long it'll take to find Susie."

"I can always have my parents wire me more."

Russell sounded like he'd rather go sit in a dentist's chair than talk to Mom and Dad, and the rattle in his right leg told Skip even more about his nerves. "You can stay here tonight, since you've already paid for it, or you can check out and come home with me." Skip came close enough to rest a hand on Russell's shoulder. The big guy could handle himself in a fight, but he wasn't used to Seattle's gritty edges. "I've got a friendly bottle and a record player. We can have a little party."

Russell's grin warmed even though he wouldn't meet Skip's gaze. "That would be real nice of you."

"What can I say?" Skip gave an exaggerated shrug. "I'm a nice guy." A nice guy who liked to live dangerously. They gave the front desk clerk Russell's key, and half an hour later, they walked up the dim hall to his apartment.

Took him three tries to open the door. Damned thing always stuck. Russell stood to one side, all but vibrating with nerves.

Between the second and third try, Skip grabbed him by the collar and gave him a kiss, stifling Russell's surprised "What?" under his lips.

"For luck." Skip raised a "don't move" finger and went back to the door.

"What if someone had seen?"

The door popped open, and Skip gave the hall an exaggerated appraisal. "No one here." He swept through the door, covering a burst of nerves with bluster. "Come on in. I won't bite." He rarely brought men home, except for Lou. His place might not be respectable enough for a college boy from the Midwest.

Russell dropped his suitcase on the floor. "Sure."

"Lemme pour drinks." Skip would only have one to be companionable. He'd made himself enough trouble stone-cold sober. He went into the kitchenette for the bottle and glasses, leaving

Russell to inspect the place.

It was only about nine in the evening, still bright enough that they didn't need the overhead lights. His studio apartment held little more than a Murphy bed, an old chair from his mother's place, some bookshelves, and a music stand. He hadn't folded the bed up before work, and it dominated the room in a sprawl of wrinkled sheets.

When he came out with the bourbon, Russell was flipping through one of his magazines.

"*Dime Western*?" Russell gave an amused huff. "You really do read this stuff."

Skip handed over the drink. "It's not nice to laugh at a man's library."

Picking up the next book in the stack, Russell read the title with a smirk. "*Locker Room Lovers*? Wait a minute." He grabbed the next one, squinting at the cover, where three men sat arm in arm on a bed. "*We Three Queens*? What is this stuff?"

Skip snatched the books. "I'll let you borrow one if you'll be nice about it."

"They actually write books about…" Russell pointed at Skip, then at himself. Skip was tired of that gesture.

"Men copping it up the back door? Yes, they write books about it." Skip tossed off a deep drink of his bourbon. He hated getting laughed at, and something better change his mood before he kicked Russell right out in the street. He wanted to help, he really did, but the guy already meant more to him than any tourist from Minnesota ought to.

He hated getting hurt even worse than getting laughed at.

"Come on," he said abruptly. "Let's dance."

"Dance?"

Skip set his glass down and went to the closet for the record player. All his 45s were in a stack in the bookcase. "Open that orange box and see what you can find."

In moments, he had a record on the turntable. He spun around to face Russell and raised his hands. "Now do you want to lead, or shall I?"

❧

"You're joking." Russell froze, trapped by what he wanted and what he thought he should do.

Skip rocked forward and back, then took three quick steps. "I promised you the cha-cha." He repeated the patter. "Come on. Step, two, cha-cha-cha." He moved in time with his words.

"I don't know."

"You can do it." Skip took two steps to the side, did a quick cha-cha-cha, then a showy turn, ending up in front of Russell. "I can see you want to."

Russell had never been so confused in his life. Losing Susie had hurt, and he shouldn't be consoling himself with someone else, especially not another man. Skip was gorgeous, though, his hair tumbling into his face, his slender body flowing through the dance moves.

He'd given up his chance to protest when he brought Skip into his hotel room.

"Final offer." Skip shimmied close enough for his woodsy aftershave to tease Russell.

If he tilted his head an inch, even less, they'd kiss. And boy howdy, Russell wanted to. Skip ran his tongue over his lower lip, and heat surged through Russell's core. He raised his hands slowly.

Each put one hand on the other's shoulder, the fingers of their free hands laced together. Their bellies were close enough to touch.

"When I step forward, you step back." Skip counted them off, and they were dancing.

"Step, two, cha-cha-cha," Russell whispered the pattern, trying to keep from stepping on Skip's toes. He felt blocky and awkward, and the growing heat in his groin made it hard to concentrate.

"Side, and," Skip said, leading Russell through the dance. Somehow Russell managed not to stumble or trip or otherwise embarrass himself. They kept going till a rough hiss from the record player marked the end of the song.

Skip disentangled his hand from Russell's. "Let me start the music again."

"No." Russell had never been a good follower, and he didn't want to dance. Hell, he wanted to bend Skip over the chair and take him, though he'd never been inside another person, either man or woman. Covering Skip's long, strong fingers with his own, Russell tugged to bring him closer.

"I could read to you from the *Three Queens* book." Skip trailed his fingers along the white stripes in Russell's shirt.

The last dregs of sunset turned the air to amber. The record player hissed and clicked as the 45 continued to spin. Nothing made sense except Skip's presence and the overwhelming urge to touch him. "One thing at a time." He brushed the barest kiss over Skip's mouth.

It was a small movement, the lightest contact imaginable, but Skip exhaled as if he'd been punched in the gut. Russell shifted his grip to the back of Skip's head, threading his fingers through his slick hair and applying more sincere attention to his lips. One of them groaned. Might have been Skip, though the sound vibrating against Russell's sternum could have come from his own heart.

They kissed, openmouthed, raw and hot and messy. After two years with Susie, where every kiss was an event, the result of careful planning and a great deal of self-persuasion, kissing Skip felt as natural as breathing.

*Susie.* Russell slammed the door on that line of thinking. His problems with her had no place here.

Working together, they unbuttoned Russell's shirt and shoved his slacks to the floor. He flexed his hips, delirious from the rough rub of Skip's dungarees against his bare cock.

Desire became a separate thing, riding Russell as surely as the other man's hands on his body. Skip worked the soft skin on his neck with his lips and his teeth and his tongue, and Russell clenched his fists, his arms tensed, his pulse racing. "You're killing me."

"I'm trying." Skip growled in his ear. "Only fair, after what you've done to me."

Russell would have asked what he meant, but Skip pulled him down for another kiss. Their lips met hard. Skip's mouth was sweet and hot and spicy, the perfect combination of supple and strong. Russell didn't ever want to come up for air, but when he did, he gasped out a compliment. "Good kisser."

"Horn player."

Skip's chuckle melted what was left of his reserve. He got an arm around Skip's waist and pulled him across the room, making them both stumble into the bed. The sheets smelled of starch and the musky pomade Skip used on his hair.

"You're wasted on the girls, lover." Skip paused in unbuttoning his shirt, giving Russell a once-over where he sprawled naked on the bed.

"Don't." Russell grabbed at the waistband of Skip's dungarees. "Just get these off and get over here."

"Whatever you say, boss."

Skip stripped off his blue jeans and crawled on top. They rocked against each other till Russell was blind to everything but the pleasure of cock thrusting against cock. He reached down and took them both in hand, bringing a grunt from Skip, his wide mouth caught in a grimace. Russell grinned and thrust harder. Skip's belly flexed, his muscles tensed.

"Enjoying yourself?" Russell asked, a mostly rhetorical question.

Skip wrapped a hand around Russell's and squeezed, tightening the pressure. "Yeah."

He licked his lips, and Russell gave in to the desire to taste him. Licking, nibbling, he worked Skip's lips and throat. His balls tightened, and he thrust feverishly into their joined hands.

"Jesus, Russell." Skip bucked against Russell's hips, once, twice, three times, and come squirted across Russell's belly. A moment later, his own climax rocked him with enough force to drag the air out of his lungs. Skip's elbow buckled, and he collapsed to one side. The only sound in the room was their heavy breathing.

Men shouted at each other out on the street, making Russell twitch. "Sorry." He eased up on one elbow and smiled down at Skip. His hair fell around his face, softening his features, and his full lips gave evidence to having been thoroughly kissed.

With a teasing smile, Skip dipped a finger in one of the smears of come and made a show of licking it clean. *Mine*, he mouthed.

"Yes," Russell whispered, pretty sure he didn't just mean the mess on his chest. After a few minutes, Skip got up for a damp towel, and they both washed off. Then they scooted around so they lay spoon style, Skip's back to Russell's front. Sated and half-asleep, Russell was aware of little more than the moonlight and Skip's soft breath.

He should probably offer to make up a bunk on the floor, since Skip's offer of a place to stay didn't necessarily include a bed. He'd do that as soon as the strength came back to his legs. Meantime, he'd make plans for finding Susie.

Any time now.

The present moment was sweet, and languor weighed down his limbs. For once, his confusion faded. The rest of the world could go to hell.

## Chapter 13

（

HEADING NORTH ON HIGHWAY 99, Skip had a solid chance of getting to work late, but he was too damned distracted to care. He cruised along through the no-man's land between Lynnwood and Everett, where scattered farms battled with the forest for control of the land, and hit most of the yellow lights when they were closer to tangerine. If he put the pedal down, he'd make it in time.

The sun sat right on top of the Cascade Mountains, splashes of lemonade and peach turning the mountains purple against a sky the clean blue of his old Schwinn bike. The night before, he'd barely been able to sleep, Russell's presence in his bed a constant tremolo at the edge of his consciousness. Reaching a light too red to run, he slowed the car and rubbed his jaw with the palm of his hand, enjoying the chapped skin from Russell's rough beard. The lack of sleep hadn't made him late. Waking up in the morning with a thick cock riding the small of his back had caused the real delay.

It had taken some coaxing, but he'd persuaded Russell to climb on top. Russell had straddled him, muscular thighs pinning his arms to his body. Skip rubbed a fingertip along his lower lip, still sore from the pounding. He loved starting the day with a dick down his throat. The other stuff? The crappy sadness he'd feel after Russell left? He'd deal with that later.

Parking the car drove his mood into the ground. The only open spaces were at the back of the lot. The old Buick choked and sputtered for twenty seconds after he killed the engine. Damned carburetor. Skip jogged toward the oversized building, debating whether he should try a side door and make excuses for punching the time clock late. In the end, he headed for the main door.

He ran straight into the crew chief.

"Johansen." Danny's tone was grim.

"Sorry, boss." Skip pulled his timecard out of the rack. "Traffic was awful."

The crew chief crossed his arms. "You're out of chances, Johansen." His scowl would have taken the fizz out of a soda pop. "Next time you come in late, you might as well go straight to the office and get your final check."

Skip stifled a joke. Not much made the guy mad, but this was close. He mumbled another apology and headed onto the factory floor, ready to sling airplane parts from one end of the building to the other. The real deal was, he hated anything and everything having to do with airplane parts, hated it almost as much as he hated the disease ruining his mother's lungs, hated it almost as much as he loved playing his horn.

If he lived in San Francisco or LA, he'd never have to look at another box of altimeters, wires sticking out the back like a swarm of insects. But if he lived in California, his mother could take a turn for the worse and be dead before he could get home.

He really didn't have much choice but to stay.

### ℭ

Russell wished he had time to laze in the sunlight filtering through the roller shades. As he lay in bed, relaxation saturated every muscle, a layer of protection against the guilt he was bound to feel. He needed to get to the hospital and check on Phyllis and he needed to find Susie. More importantly, he needed to forget last night, the dancing, the laughter, and all that went with it.

The first step toward forgetting was a slow climb out of bed. He sponged off, doggedly unwilling to shower away Skip's touch. The scent of Skip's pomade clung to Russell's skin. He wanted it there, though it would make the forgetting more difficult.

The photographs on the walls of Skip's tiny apartment didn't help either. Skip on stage, trim and handsome in a black tuxedo. Skip laughing, surrounded by Lulu and her friends. Skip standing next to an older woman whose frailty enhanced her exquisite beauty.

Sitting on the edge of the bed, the sheets pungent with sex, Russell's scattered recollections brought on another raging hard-on.

Time to go.

Skip's tiny kitchen was pretty much empty of real food. Pocketing the spare key, Russell strode briskly down the hall to the building's main entrance, past a man who stood in the doorway fixing a vacancy sign to a fancy wrought-iron frame.

"Excuse me." Russell intended to ask for directions to the hospital and a coffee shop. He had thirty-seven dollars left, and while Skip's generosity meant he wouldn't be spending money on a hotel room, some breakfast would help Russell come up with a plan.

The man, a scarecrow-type constructed exclusively of planes and angles, stopped his project and gave Russell a friendly enough smile. "Yes?"

Instead of directions, Russell asked a different question. "Your vacancy... What size is the apartment?" He'd never seriously consider moving to Seattle, but just this once, he'd let his curiosity win.

The man pushed up the sloppy sleeves of his plaid shirt. "One bedroom. You want to see it?"

Russell offered the man his hand. "Sure."

The man introduced himself as the building manager, and Russell followed him back inside, nodding in agreement at every one of the apartment's selling points. They climbed the carpeted stairs to the third floor. Some of the apartments they passed were quiet, but others nearly exploded with the unchecked enthusiasm of young children. They saw other tenants, most of them men, but a few women. With their baby buggies and knee-high kids, they personified the future he'd anticipated for him and Susie.

The future they'd spent the last two weeks dismantling.

"Are you a single man, or is there a missus somewhere?" Eyeing Russell with curiosity, the manager pulled a large loop of keys off his belt and flipped through them.

Russell had to clear his throat before he could respond. "Single."

The man nodded. "Well, this'un's a one bedroom, but I might have a studio opening up soon."

*A studio.* A premonition of loneliness settled into Russell's belly.

The vacant apartment was larger than Skip's, the windows overlooking the fire station across the street. The wood floors had scuffed trails leading from room to room and the kitchen was separated by a set of glass-paneled doors. The early morning sunlight gave the room a warm glow, inviting happiness.

When the building manager told him the monthly rent was seventy-five dollars, Russell had to fight to keep his jaw from dropping. "I know. I know." The building manager patted Russell on the shoulder as if they were long-time friends. "It's a lot of money, but look at the size of the place." He gestured around the small living room. "We've got a telephone in every apartment and a big antenna on the roof so our television reception is great. Come see the bedroom."

Obediently, Russell followed him into a smaller room. The one window overlooked a dim alley, and the room was furnished with a nice-sized double bed. Room enough for two. He and Susie would have fit right in, and on a lawyer's salary, he could even have afforded the place.

The building manager kept on talking. "Now some of our tenants double up, share the space and split the rent."

Skip's taste, of spice and faded cigarettes, flooded Russell's consciousness. His cheeks heated as if the building manager could see right into his mind and know the depravity hidden there. He floundered in a rising flood of frustration, angry at himself for wasting the man's time. He'd been dumped by his girl, and instead of trying to find her, he'd given in to stupid fantasies.

Grown adult men didn't play house.

"These apartments go fast, so you let me know if you're interested," the manager said, offering Russell his hand. Russell took it, too agitated to offer more than a cursory good-bye. He escaped the apartment, escaped the building, and took off blindly.

After a breakfast tasting mostly of grease, Russell made change for a dollar and used a payphone to call every Ryker in the phone book. When that didn't work, he found a liquor store and bought a bottle of whiskey. Rationally, he should wire his parents for money and find another hotel.

He just wasn't feeling very rational.

❦

Skip hated playing with Nicky Bender, but it was a paying gig, and money was money. He'd been hired for three sets at the Camlin Hotel's Cloud Room, across the street from the Paramount Theater. He liked the space okay. The acoustics weren't too bad, and there was a nice view from eleven stories above the Denny Regrade. Big windows overlooked a warren of city lights, the top edge of the neon sign on the Paramount splashed cherry-red light on the wall, and the servers had a quick hand with the soda water whenever he raised an eyebrow. Nicky was a grody little greaser, but Skip could put up with him for a chance to play with a trio.

He unpacked his horn, rubbing smudges off the bell with a soft cloth and blowing through the mouthpiece to clear out any crud. The small stage held a piano, a drum kit, a microphone, and a stool. He set his case on a nearby table so he'd be able to grab his mute when he needed it. The good thing was, Nicky would expect him to use the mute, to mimic Chet Baker's West Coast cool style.

"So, Johansen, you're going to sing tonight, right?" Nicky's whiny nasal voice flipped him like a bonk on the funny bone. The bad thing was, the dork expected him to sing.

"Why do you want my raspy voice on the mic?"

"Because you're the only one of us who can sing in tune."

"Most of the time." Skip set aside his horn and propped himself with both hands on the stool. "Sure. I'll sing."

"How 'bout five songs over the night?"

*Well, I wouldn't want to interfere with your piano solos, would I.* "You're the boss."

Nicky gave him a smarmy salesman smile. "Write 'em on the set list."

Shaking his head, Skip grabbed the stub of a

pencil and thought through the list of tunes he knew. "Misty." "My Funny Valentine." "Do Nothing Till You Hear From Me." He grinned and wrote down "I've Got the World on a String," the first song Russell sang the night of the jam. Maybe he'd convince him to sing it here tonight.

If he showed up.

All day, Skip had wrestled with nerves. He liked Russell too much, and sometimes the man returned the favor. When he wasn't fussing about some woman or his own inclinations. If by some miracle Russell decided to stick around, one of those was bound to trip them up.

Skip tried to ignore his lousy mood. Getting nailed by his supervisor hadn't helped. He sucked in a breath, fighting the way his gut squirmed. He'd left Russell with a key and a list of places Ryker liked to hang out, and the other man promised he'd find his way here.

Skip couldn't do anything except wonder. He would show tonight. He had to.

Three hours later, Skip was still wondering.

The room had filled with people drawn in by Nicky Bender's reputation for quality jazz. The soft, steady, murmur of conversation ebbed and flowed like waves under the music, though Skip struggled to keep his mind on his playing. Far too often, his attention wandered to the doorway, to the shadowy areas of the room, as if Russell had snuck in and hidden from him on purpose.

No luck.

Near the end of the third set, Nicky called for "My Funny Valentine." Skip adjusted the mute covering the bell of his trumpet, then gently blew the opening notes. He had a few solo measures before Nicky joined on the piano. The sad, sweet phrases perfectly echoed Skip's frame of mind. When it came to his physical needs, he took care of business easily enough, but he held most guys off with a slippery smile and empty promises. Not this time. Russell had so much confidence, so much strength, but his need called to Skip like neon through the fog.

Damn the man. Skip wanted to hold out his hand and draw Russell in and make him feel safe. The buzz of his horn against his lips reminded him of the rough heat of Russell's kiss, melancholy and oh so sweet. The band finished the first time through the melody. Time to sing.

He lowered the horn. Stepped to the microphone. Inhaled. Skip's voice didn't match the beauty of his trumpet's tone, but he knew the trick of letting the truth come through the words. From the crowd's hush, he could tell he'd grabbed them, and for the first time all night, he let go. Uncertainty, sadness, and longing seeped into the phrases. The piano and drums created a steady foundation for his testimony, the forty people in the seats his witnesses.

He stared at nothing, let the music take over. Glanced up.

Russell stood in the doorway, jacket unbuttoned, hands shoved in his trousers pockets.

The weight of his gaze stripped Skip naked, and he had to pull back from the microphone, let the horn finish the verse. Then the piano took over, and he could step back even further, only responsible for ornamenting the piano's lead. A waitress directed Russell to a table near the window to Skip's left. Russell found something fascinating outside, barely acknowledging the pretty young woman who handed him a highball half-full of amber liquid. His jaw was hard, and he tapped the table with one finger, not quite matching the drummer's beat.

Skip knew all this because for the final three songs in the set, he hadn't been able to take his eyes off the table near the window to his left. Not that it was any big secret, but he was gone on Russell. The strength of his feeling made him draw in, close down. It turned his playing tentative and the crowd noise rose as if they all could tell how much he held back.

Still, people were polite and used applause to encourage an encore. Nicky called for "Lover Man," a bluesy old Billie Holiday song. The slow and mournful phrases allowed Skip to tell Russell exactly how he felt.

If Russell was listening.

*Shut up. No more paranoia talking. The man's here, isn't he?*

The final notes were lost in a swell of applause. Once talking and laughter replaced the applause, Skip packed his gear, moving slowly, deliberately, forcing his nerves in line. The restaurant's manager brought Nicky an envelope, and before he left the stage, Skip went over to get his share of the night's take. Eight dollars. Union scale. Nicky asked him about an upcoming date, and Skip agreed without checking his calendar. Russell was paying his bill, and Skip's heart dropped lower than the hotel lobby, afraid Russell would leave without even saying good night.

Crazy thoughts, because Russell still had his spare key.

Tension buzzed through Skip like a hi-hat going double time. He flipped the hair out of his face and did his best to act casual. He sidled between the tables, attention on the back of the room, where a haze of cigarette smoke shadowed the bar. He shot quick glances at Russell, who sat with his elbows on the table, fingers interlaced, one thumbnail caught between his teeth. Getting a hold of that mouth, those knuckles, would do a lot toward changing Skip's mood, though the flat withdrawal in Russell's eyes made him doubt he'd ever get the chance.

"I knew you were good." Russell tipped his chin, adjusted his shoulders, shook out his hands. "I was wrong."

Skip was slow to pull out a chair, slower still to sit. Russell's mouth was relaxed, but his eyes were hot, angry, hungry.

"You're not just good," Russell continued. "You're an artist." He placed his hands carefully on the table, palms down, fingers spread. "You're a genius."

Skip settled into the chair, nodding at the empty highball on the table. "How much have you had to drink?"

Russell's eyelids slid to half-mast, and his grin wiped away most of his anger and tension, leaving only heat and hunger. "Whiskey was cheaper than food."

He spoke softly, but the waitress chose right then to lean over his shoulder and set some change on the table. Russell's gaze dropped to the floor, and his cheeks flushed. Before Skip could figure out what was bugging him, a commotion in the doorway drew his attention.

Marquise Johnson stood, fussing at one of the waiters. "Yes, I know y'all are closing, but I need to see Mr. Johansen. He's right over there."

After a moment, the waiter gave up and let Marquise in. He sauntered over to their table, tall and lanky and as nelly as any man in the city. On bass or rhythm guitar, the guy kept time like a metronome. He'd been the heartbeat of too many bands for most musicians to pay attention to his eccentricities.

The throbbing pulse in Russell's jaw told Skip his visitor wouldn't cut Marquise the same slack.

"Darling!" Marquise crowed when he got close to their table. His name suggested he had some colored blood, but his skin was as fair as Skip's.

Skip couldn't keep from grinning at the other man's flouncing steps. "I haven't seen you in forever, man. What are you doing here?"

Marquise spun a chair around and straddled it, facing Russell and Skip. "You been holding out on us, Skippy. Who's your new friend?"

Something cracked over in Russell's direction, and Skip hoped it was a knuckle and not a molar. "This is Russell. He's just visiting from the Midwest." And from the look on his face, he couldn't run home fast enough. Skip exhaled hard. Geez, but he was tired of Russell's moods. "You didn't answer my question, Keezy. You should have come by earlier. We could have used you up there tonight."

"Nah." Marquise waved a graceful hand, and Russell eased back in his chair.

"I heard from old Diller down at the Double Header that he heard from Sven Michaelson's piano player that you were looking for Ryker."

Skip blinked, tracking the connections. "You know where he is?"

"I do indeed." Marquise pursed his lips, as if he might tease Skip for the information.

Russell's chair scraped across the floor, hard enough to be rude. "'Scuse me. I'll be, uh, back." The wobble in his step tempted Skip to go after him, at least for the half a second it took anger to spark. Nope, the big guy would have to figure things out for himself. Skip crossed one leg over the other. Yeah, it was a swishy pose. He was a swishy guy. Let Russell chew on that for a while.

"Skippy?" Marquise patted him on the shoulder. "I heard about your new boyfriend too."

Skip bit his lip to keep from saying something snappy. Of course people would talk.

"My friend, you have got your hands full, don't you." Marquise's pat turned into a shoulder rub. "But Lordy, what a ride that would be."

Skip rocked his head back, eyes shut, fighting a laugh. "Shut your trap, Keezy." He sat up abruptly. "Wait, don't shut it. Tell me where Ryker is."

Before he answered, Russell stumbled back from the direction of the bathroom. "I should go."

Skip half stood, reaching out a hand in case Russell went over. "Hang on, buddy." He shot a glance at Marquise. "Where?"

After a suggestive lick across his lower lip, Marquise answered. "Word from the bird is he's out at his cabin in Long Beach. You know where that is, right?" He rose and spun the chair the right way around. "And now, as much as I'd love to stick around and help you two lovers find your way home, I'm going to leave you to your own devices."

His laughter trailed behind the swing in his step.

"I'm fine." Russell's words had more of a slur than before.

"You're drunk." Skip picked up his horn. "Come on. We'll grab a bite at the Dog House and get some sleep. I think I have a plan for this weekend."

Russell raised a finger as if he were posing an argument in a court of law, but Skip brushed past him before he could get any words out.

He stopped about three tables away. "Come on, hero."

Skip left without checking to see whether Russell followed him.

They met at the elevator.

Riding down eleven floors, just the two of them in a cramped space, spawned so much tension, the car could have bounced when it hit the lobby. Skip led the way to the Buick, unlocking Russell's door before stowing his horn in the trunk.

"I promised myself I wouldn't come home with you tonight," Russell said again as soon as Skip climbed into the driver's seat.

Skip slammed his door but otherwise didn't comment. Right then he was too angry to save Russell from himself. A smart guy would drop this punk at the closest hotel and lay a patch on the street out front.

Maybe Skip was a fool, but he wanted to believe that with a little time, Russell would get over Susie and return his feelings. Skip wouldn't allow himself to be treated badly forever, but… "I must be a glutton for punishment, because we're taking a road trip."

The change in subject jerked Russell's chain. He sat with his arms across his chest, jaw tight, knuckles blanching.

"What?"

"Marquise just said they're out in Long Beach." Skip couldn't keep the bite out of his voice.

Russell grabbed the dash hard enough to leave scuff marks with his fingernails. "California?"

"There's a Long Beach, Washington too, and I'm offering to drive you out there this weekend." He paused long enough to roll down the window. "But not if you're going to be a jerk."

"Jesus, I'm sorry." Russell flopped back against the seat and raked his fingers through his hair. "I'm being an idiot. Sure, we can go. Phyllis's parents are here, so I won't need to hang around the hospital anymore."

Skip put his blinker on again. The Dog House was only a few blocks from the Camlin, which was good because the short distance made it less likely he'd toss Russell out on the street.

He parked the car, reaching over to take one of Russell's hands in his. "We're going to eat, and then we're going to go home and go to sleep, you drunken idiot."

Russell rubbed his mouth with his free hand, his normal self-assurance faded to nothing. This soft side of Russell sucked Skip in even harder.

"If I don't get food and some coffee into you, you're going to be sick in the morning."

Russell's smile was weak, dragging Skip in a little further.

"I've got a stake in this too." Skip twisted his fingers through Russell's, keeping their hands low, chagrined at how good the contact felt. "We've got a gig Monday night. If Ryker's really out in Long Beach, I'm going to haul his butt back home."

"I sure appreciate what you're doing." Russell spoke to the floor, his voice gruff.

His grip was so warm and tight, Skip could barely breathe. "Good."

# Chapter 14

((

RUSSELL WOKE UP, ALONE IN the bed except for his headache. Between the throbbing vise behind his eyes and the wicked grip of nausea, it was just as well he didn't have company. While he debated when and how far to move, the bracing scent of coffee gave him the energy to pry an eyelid open. The glare from the windows slammed it shut.

"Coffee?" Skip's voice came from the other side of the room.

With a groan, Russell rolled onto his back, forearm covering his eyes. He didn't know what to say. With consciousness came patchy memories, filtered through a layer of embarrassment. Who knew what he'd really done the night before, besides act like a jackass.

"I owe you…" He tried to apologize but his throat was scratchy and the words clumped together. He'd pay for his whiskey dinner, but letting Skip down made it worse.

"Didn't quite catch that."

Something in Skip's voice made him brave the

morning sun. Annoyance, verging on anger. Russell gritted his teeth and propped himself on his elbows. "I'm sorry about last night." The room swayed in time with the throbbing in his head.

Skip sat at the tiny dining table, painfully framed by a window's glare. "You ought to be."

Russell gave up and flopped onto the mattress. "Thank you for taking care of me." And for the place to stay, and for giving him something to think about besides his girlfriend.

Ex-girlfriend.

*The hell with it.* Thinking took too much trouble, and feeling made everything worse. Russell swung his legs over the edge of the bed and managed to sit without upchucking. Didn't care if keeping his back to his host was rude. "I'll get out of your hair." Self-pity was so manly. "I'm sure you have plans for today."

Skip's snort was underlined by the scrape of his chair on the wood floor. "Yep. I'm driving out to the coast because Keezy says Ryker's gone on the lam and I worked too hard lining up Monday's gig to call in a sub now." His heavy footsteps crossed the floor. "If you want to tag along, you'd be welcome."

"Not sure there's much point." Russell dropped his head in his hands, resisting the urge to reach out for Skip. "I don't really imagine Susie'll want to talk to me anyway."

"I wondered about that."

"I have to do something, though." *Don't be a whiner, Haunreiter.* "I doubt she'll listen to logic, so I'd thought to appeal to her sense of responsibility, tell her she's letting down her family and leaving her friends on the team in the lurch." He absolutely wouldn't mention anything to do with their relationship.

The silence grew long enough, Russell dared a glance around. Skip stood close, a puzzled smile on his face. Maybe he wasn't too mad. Relief danced through the fog in Russell's mind. "Do you always take in strays like this?" he muttered, finding another reason to be embarrassed.

Skip perched next to him on the bed. "They say it's because I'm in touch with my womanly side."

The tilt of Skip's head combined with an exaggerated lisp had Russell fighting a smile. "You mean like…" He rubbed his eyes, trying to get the words right. Ever since meeting Lulu, he'd wondered. "Your friend there, the, uh, woman who gave me your phone number."

"Nah, not like Lulu." Humor slid through the sound of Skip's voice, and for the first time all morning, Russell took a deep breath.

"Go take a shower." Skip gave his thigh a comforting pat. "A cup of coffee and you'll be right as rain."

Russell nodded, planted his hands on his knees, and forced himself to stand. At least now he only had a headache and queasy stomach to worry about.

☙

"Are you ready, Freddy?" Skip grinned, a little tentative since he wasn't sure which Russell Haunreiter would answer, the prissy Midwesterner or the one who could make the three queens blush. Skip chalked up Russell's moodiness to the drink. He didn't want to think too much about the reasons for his own moodiness. They had a couple of hours on the road, and Skip hoped he'd find some reason to finally convince himself Russell wasn't worth all the trouble.

"Let's go." Russell shifted in his seat, stretched his legs out as far as they would go. Plenty far.

Skip pinched the tip of his tongue between his teeth, a shot of pain to keep him from thinking about where he wanted those legs and the body that came with them.

Down in the Square, the bright noon sunshine pushed the thermometer past eighty and showed off every dirty corner. A drunk curled in a doorway, either asleep or passed out, the glass windows on either side of him boarded over and the door itself nailed shut with two-by-fours. Most of the bars and restaurants were closed, but a grocery store was open, and a few stragglers navigated the broken sidewalks, either leftovers from last night or getting an early start.

When they drove past the tavern, Russell straightened. "This place is rougher than I thought."

"But it's home."

The big guy's deep chuckle went straight to Skip's groin. Russell shifted in the seat to lean against the door, his smile a halfway dare. "So how long will it take to get to Long Beach?"

Skip ran his gaze over Russell's body. "About two hours, maybe three. We'll have to turn it around quick, because I do want to get back in time to visit with Mom tomorrow."

"And you know where this cabin is?"

"I've been there before." Skip patted his shirt pocket.

Out on the highway, Russell's gaze prickled Skip's right side the way the hot sun beat on his left. Highway 99 ran along the waterfront, a blur of train cars and shipping containers. Farther south, it passed through neighborhoods with small shops and motor hotels, their neon signs glowing dully in the glaring sun.

After about an hour, they stopped at a market for a Coke. The small space was crowded with shelves holding products Skip had heard about on the radio, the kind where laughing announcers promised miracles for free.

In real life, they all had a price tag.

Russell stood by a rack holding small packages of chips. From behind him, Skip rested a hand on his shoulder.

Russell stiffened, turned his head, shot a glance at Skip's hand. Stepped away. Eyes flashed in the direction of the cash register.

Skip crossed his arms and covered his smile with one hand. "You wanted a Coke too, right?"

"What?" Russell snapped as if Skip had asked him to strip in the middle of the shop.

"A Coke?" Skip backed up a step, then two, lips still twitching with the urge to laugh. "I'll see you at the cash register." He grabbed a couple of bottles of soda and waited for the antique behind the counter to ring him up. He gave her a quarter, and she gave him back a dime and a nickel. Russell stood behind him, a solid mass of unhappiness. Skip let him stew.

*Serves him right.*

There. He had a reason. Russell was too uptight. They'd never last. He headed for the car with Russell still standing by the Ivory Snow. Pulling the car into the gas station next door, Skip still couldn't figure out whether he should laugh or get mad. By the time Russell joined him, Russell's head was hanging, and he didn't make eye contact.

That decided things. Skip had always been a sucker for a lost puppy.

The silence between them had lost its easy feeling, replaced with something else. Skip did his best to stifle his impatience, but it rattled his innards, ready to spill out of his mouth at the slightest prompting. He pulled onto Highway 99, and when they reached a red light, he passed Russell a Coke.

"So…" Didn't take much for Skip to run out of things to say.

"I'm sorry."

"You're doing it again." He spat the words, then blew out a heavy breath. He never snapped. Russell was driving him crazy.

"Doing what?"

Skip fingered a precise B-flat scale along the steering wheel. "Apologizing."

"I'm…shit." Russell pressed an open palm to his forehead. For a big, strong man, he could be an awful baby sometimes.

Looking for his bottle opener, Skip reached across Russell's lap and popped open the glove compartment. "Listen," he said, pinning the soda between his knees. "I didn't mean to bug you." He flipped off the metal bottle top, eyes on the road, every other sense locked on Russell. "Men touch each other, you know?"

"Yeah." Russell held out his hand for the bottle opener. "But what if the shopkeeper had guessed?"

Now Skip couldn't help but laugh. "Guessed what? That old fossil couldn't remember her own name, let alone worry about us."

Russell opened his soda, not smiling but no longer looking so constipated.

"We'll make a deal." Skip choked back a laugh. "I won't touch you in public and—"

"I'll try not to act like an idiot." Russell raised his Coke in toast.

Skip clicked his bottle against Russell's.

"I do worry, though." Russell paused to take a sip of his soda, his gaze far away. "There was a fellow from school, not a friend, you know, but someone I knew, and he was discovered in, well, an indiscreet situation." He took another swallow, his voice ever more remote. "He's at the funny farm now, getting shock treatments."

Skip dragged the hair out of his face. "Cool it, pops. You're bringing me down."

"It's true. You greasers laugh at the rules, but that cop down at the warehouse sure knew your name well enough."

The urge to guffaw fought with sincere anger. "First of all, Daddy-O, I am *not* a greaser. The hardest drug I take is vodka, and I shower at least once a week. Secondly, Murphy's worked down in the Square since I was in high school. If he was going

to arrest me, he'd a done it by now. And third…"
He didn't finish the thought. He'd never met a
man who tore him up this bad.

They drove past a Texaco, a burger joint, and
the Larchmont Motel. Chuck Berry came on the
radio, and Skip turned the music up. Fight him or
fuck him, it was all the same right now.

❦

They hit Long Beach at about ten miles per
hour, following a long line of cars up Pacific Avenue. The slow pace gave Russell plenty of time to
worry about what would happen when they found
Susie.

With one hand loose on the steering wheel,
Skip took a swallow of his fourth Coke since they'd
hit the road. "Looks like we're stuck in Antsville."

"Busier than I thought it'd be." Russell rode
with his elbow propped on the open car window,
taking in the sights. Between the sun-burnished
copper lights in Skip's hair and the easy charm in
his smile, Russell figured it was safer to keep his
eyes on the road.

Skip's gift for pouring soul into his music was
matched by his free and easy laugh. By his generosity. His warmth. Impressions more than full ideas
flashed through Russell's mind, leaving him with
the bone-deep certainty that he wouldn't go home
unchanged.

"Lots of people on summer vacation."

Russell dared a glance in his direction. "Thought
you said you'd been here before."

"Yeah, but it's been a couple years."

*His smile.* Cocky, but sweet enough to take the sting away. So easy to return, with interest. Flustered, Russell pointed out his window. "Do you see the big frying pan? Must be fifteen feet tall."

Skip snickered. "I'm busy watching out for Jake the Alligator Man over here."

Russell whipped around and caught the word "museum" on the side of a building. This town had all sorts of tourist attractions.

Their gazes met. Russell ducked, turned, his jaw tight and his cheeks hot. They rolled past low houses on small lots with trim yards and piles of geraniums. After the dustup coming out of Olympia, they'd settled into an easy rapport, some talk, some quiet, and an unspoken need confining itself to quick glances and slow smiles. Russell took in a slow, deep breath. He should be worried about Susie, not Skip.

*Now don't louse things up.*

He wasn't at all sure which one he feared lousing things up with.

Cars were parked solid along both sides of the street, electrical wires tangled above them, and the smell of saltwater dominated everything. Overhead, the clarion-blue sky was enormous, and Russell tried not to gawk.

On the other side of town, traffic died away. The road wound up into the hills, giving them snapshots of the ocean through stands of evergreen trees. After another mile or so, they took a right off the highway. Ryker's place was one of six identical white cottages lining a circular drive. The cottages faced a deep green lawn, and more evergreens crowded around their shoulders. They had tiny porches and blue front doors, and their eaves were trimmed with white-painted curlicues.

"All they need is a pack of dwarves," Skip muttered.

Russell snorted.

Several cars were parked on the gravel strip between driveway and lawn, roughly matched with individual cabins. Skip pulled the old Buick behind a Cadillac and took the slip of paper with the address from his pocket. "Says it's number four."

Russell opened his door, nerves twisted tight, the band of muscle across his shoulders even tighter. He'd had hours to come up with the clincher, the one thing that would bring Susie home, and instead he'd spent the time mooning over Skip.

Aunt Maude was going to have a cow.

"That's his car," Skip said.

The grim set to Skip's jaw surprised Russell, because he'd half thought the musician's line about dragging his drummer home was just that, a line. An excuse for a road trip. He looked pretty darned serious now, though. Russell straightened slowly, marshalling his arguments.

Skip got out of the Buick, and together they climbed onto the porch. The late-afternoon light slanted across the clearing, the air so still, he could hear the trees growing.

Russell knocked.

A brief scramble of footsteps and whispers were cut off with a stifled shriek. Then nothing. Skip stood beside him, muttering about lame drummers, breathing loud.

Russell knocked a second time, hard enough to rattle the door on its hinges. "We know you're in there. It's Russell and Skip. Open the damned door."

More whispers, and the door cracked open. A disembodied voice called out, "What do you want?"

"What do we want?" Shoving past him, Skip hit the door hard and forced it open. "I don't know apples from oranges, but I think the big guy here wants to settle a grudge." He kept going till he was nose to nose with Ryker. "I did tell him not to break your hands so you can play the drums on Monday."

"Aw, shut up," Ryker said. He was shirtless, his dungarees worn and patched on one knee. Susie stood behind him with a death grip on his elbow. Her fingernails were painted bright red, and the neckline of her light cotton shift showed more skin that Russell had ever seen.

She looked fast and fierce, and the confidence in the way she touched Ryker brought the morning's nausea rushing back. Russell flexed his fist.

Hitting the creep might make him feel better.

"Back off, Russell," Susie snapped. She edged closer to Ryker, and he wrapped an arm around her waist. "You are *not* going to hit him."

"He might." Skip slid his gaze in Russell's direction, his smile an invitation to keep up the act. Russell did, flaring out his chest and cracking his knuckles. Violence hadn't been on his list of arguments, but neither was finding Susie in some kind of sex pit. For the moment, he'd stick with what was working.

"He was pretty cranked up in the car." Skip underscored the threat with a nonchalant toss of his head.

Russell took a step forward. Both Ryker and Susie hopped back. Then she came at him and speared him in the chest with a blood-red talon. "Cut it out, Russell Haunreiter. I broke up with you fair and square, and now Ryker and I are getting married."

Her words sucked the air right out of the room. *Married?* He blinked once and flexed his fists for real. "What'd your Mom say when you told her that?"

Susie crossed her arms, lower lip thrust forward. "None of your business."

Anger, hot and ready, surged through him. "You have told her, right?" Russell might not have been the best boyfriend, but he did care for Susie, and he didn't want to see her throw her life away. He took a solid step in Ryker's direction.

This time, Skip slowed him down with a firm grip on his upper arm. "Whoa, boy, simmer down. I meant it when I said I need him to play the drums on Monday."

"Man, I told Paddy you needed to find a substitute," Ryker whined, getting between Russell and Susie. Russell choked back a laugh. *At least he's man enough to come out from behind her skirts.*

"There's not enough time." Skip's face turned red, and Russell hoped he'd never be on the other end of that glare. "They hired the combo, and we're all going to be there. Besides." Skip cocked his head at Russell, as if they were having a private conversation. "If this chicky's parents show up, aren't you going to want to be home in Seattle where Daddy can help?"

"Show up?" Susie squeaked.

Ryker wrapped an arm around her shoulders. "They won't call your parents."

"I guess we won't." Russell shrugged, struggling to keep the excitement off his face. Skip had just handed him the clincher. "But Aunt Maude changed our tickets so we can go right on to Detroit. You take the train with me Wednesday morning, and I'll forget to say anything."

"What?" Susie's outrage all but cracked a window. Russell felt slimy for bribing her, but he needed to get her on the train and didn't guess appealing to her sense of responsibility would work. If she'd told her parents, he wouldn't have stooped so low, but she hadn't, and that worried him.

Ryker stroked Susie's arm. "Don't listen to his garbage, sugar pie."

Russell wanted to break his hand.

"Sounds like a reasonable offer to me." Skip wandered farther into the room, past an antique love seat. He stopped at the window, peering out the lace curtains like he was expecting someone else to show up. "And if you come back for the gig, Ryker, I won't remind Russ here to make a phone call back home."

"You dirty bastard." Ryker spat the words.

Skip didn't blink. "Yup. Though if my mama ever hears you say that, we'll have words."

"Just get out of here. Go back to wherever you

came from," Susie said, almost incandescent with anger and fear and defiance.

Russell debated his next move. The longer they stood there yapping, the harder Susie would dig in her heels. He didn't know much about all this love stuff, but Susie sure was worked up. If he and Skip left, that'd give Ryker and Susie a chance to decide on their own whether to show up for the gig Monday night. If they showed, after she'd had time to think about what Russell had said, it'd give him another chance to talk her onto the train.

If they didn't show, Russell could tell Aunt Maude he'd done his best, short of tying Susie up and dragging her home. And as much as it frightened him, Susie would have to lie in the bed she'd made.

"Come on," he said to Skip, his decision made. "Let's get out of here."

Raking the hair out of his face, Skip gave Ryker one more scowl. "If you aren't there on Monday, I'll make damned sure everyone in town knows you're a welcher." He brushed past Russell on his way out the door.

Russell followed, pausing in the open doorway. "Susie, I know you won't believe this, but I do want you to be happy. If you and Ryker are meant to be together, finishing up the shows in Detroit won't delay things that much."

After one last look, he left. She'd turned her back to him, wrapped up in Ryker's embrace.

# Chapter 15

（

THE ROAD TO SEATTLE TOOK them back through Long Beach. Just as many tourists packed the streets, but the late-afternoon sun brushed everything with gold. "Hey, there's a parking spot coming up." The turmoil in Russell's gut made it hard to sit still. "Let's stow this thing and walk around some." He needed to shake off the dregs of Susie's sadness.

He also needed to come to terms with his own scumbag behavior.

Skip tapped his thumbs on the wheel as if playing a tune no one could hear. "Maybe we can grab some dinner."

"I'm buying." Russell shifted in his seat to keep his knee from bouncing. He probably would have to wire his parents for money, but he owed Skip a meal, and *dammit*, he was man enough to do that much.

Skip flipped on the blinker, easing to a stop when a family crossed in front of the car, mother, father, and three kids following along like a line of ducklings. "Sure." His half smile asked Russell a question. "Let's go see the ocean."

Out on the street, they mingled with the crowds. They walked past the Sands Theater, the Ocean View Hotel, the Sea Food Café, The Tides, everything named after the beach, although from the sidewalk on Pacific Avenue, they couldn't see the water.

Skip kept a good foot between them, which Russell appreciated. He had enough on his mind without the distraction brought on by the scent and the warm memories of the other man's long, lean body.

They came to an intersection with a drugstore on one corner and an old hotel on the other.

"Down there." Skip pointed in the direction of the beach and jogged across the road. Russell followed quickly to avoid oncoming traffic. Soon they reached rolling, grassy dunes. Fat clouds hung down over the horizon, and the muted rumble of the ocean found an answering echo in Russell's heart. Seeing the Pacific for the first time might not have been love at first sight, but it sure as hell was infatuation.

The road petered out into sand, and above their heads, a tapered white arch spanned the last stretch of pavement.

Black painted letters spread across the arch. *World's Longest Beach.*

A brisk breeze came straight off the ocean, spraying them with fine sand. Skip led the way between the dunes creating a knee-high barrier between town and surf. Sand filled Russell's loafers, and he paused for a moment to slip out of his shoes and to give himself a chance to get his bearings.

They stopped to let a car drive past on the hard-packed sand. "This isn't what I imagined." Russell snorted at his own understatement.

"You ever been to the ocean before?" Skip strolled over to a grassy hillock, too solitary to be called a sand dune, and flopped down.

His casual grace grabbed Russell even harder than the endless stretch of ocean the same color blue as the sky. "This is amazing. I never want to leave."

Skip chuckled. "So stay."

For a second, Russell thought he meant more than just one night. He let the word drift, concentrating on the rolled-up hems of his khaki trousers, giving himself something to look at besides Skip. They were going to have to figure out a plan for the night. Somehow he'd thought they'd be giving Susie a ride. Being alone with Skip in a hotel room near the beach seemed a lot more personal than staying at his apartment.

Russell scratched the back of his sweaty neck. He'd made a mess of things.

A strong gust sent Skip's hair tumbling into his face. He hoisted a piece of driftwood worn smooth by wind and waves. "We can always drive back to-night."

Grateful, Russell nodded at the horizon. "That'd be good."

Snapping off a mottled bit of bark, Skip threw the wood into the sand, his mouth tight. "For that matter, we can leave now."

"I do want to buy you dinner." Russell tried not

to let Skip's eagerness to leave bother him. "What's the problem?"

Skip rested his elbows on his knees, legs crossed Indian-style. "I don't know if a man's ever bought me dinner before." He chucked the wood into a clump of grass. "It might mean something more than you want it to."

Russell eased back onto his elbows, staring out over the waves. *What would it mean, exactly?* The sun was hot, but the steady wind cooled him and muffled their conversation. "I'm sorry about last night. The whiskey got the better of me."

"But do *you* want to get the better of me?" Skip's devilish grin brought heat to Russell's cheeks. This was not the way he wanted the conversation to go.

"I'm only here for another few days." He linked his fingers and reached his hands over his head as high as possible, knocking out some of his tightness with a long, slow, stretch.

"Before you go back home to find a replacement for Susie? Because if you were hoping for a reconciliation, I'd say you're stuck in Nowheresville."

Skip's comment stung, all right. Russell dropped back in the sand. A gull made a lazy circle overhead. "I guess I deserved that."

"What do any of us deserve?" Skip stretched out next to him. "You didn't deserve to have your girl run off with someone new, no more than I deserved to have my drummer skip out of town."

The gull swooped down low over the water. "I guess they didn't deserve to have us blackmailing them either." Russell choked on a lingering sense of guilt. He really wasn't the kind of man who put the screws to his friends. "You sure you're not a beatnik?"

"Shut up."

Unable to stand the thoughts in his head, Russell scrambled to his feet. "I'm going for a walk." He strode off, trudging through the white dunes, finding his footing where the sand turned dark from moisture. Susie had to take the train with him. She had to.

*And then what?* Would he really go back home and find a replacement, like Skip said? He walked until Skip was just a dot on the beach, then turned around and came back. The exercise calmed him but did nothing to straighten out his thoughts. The closest he came to a conclusion was to be square with Susie when he saw her again, and to keep his hands to himself after he and Skip had dinner.

Whether or not he found a new girlfriend back home, adding to his list of sins wouldn't help anything.

When he got back to the dune, the sun beat down and the soft sound of Skip's snores echoed the waves. Russell poked him. "Are you awake?"

Skip blinked, coughed, and sat up. "I am now."

"Will you join me for dinner if I promise not to be a jerk afterwards?"

Skip rubbed his jaw, drawing Russell's attention to the late-day shadow. "If you're a jerk, you're walking back to Seattle."

❦

Turned out the tourists had booked every room

in town, so after an awkward dinner, they hit the road. Sometime after midnight, Skip pulled into a place called the Hop-In Grocer, just north of Olympia. The grocery was dark except for the red neon glare of the Hop-In sign.

Skip tipped his head against the seat. His eyes closed on their own, giving in to the waves of sleep he'd been fighting for the last seven or eight miles.

Russell sat up straighter and cleared his throat. Red neon light washed over his cheek. Skip curled his fingers to keep from running them along the vulnerable, open stretch of skin. He just needed to get them home safe without any shenanigans. He liked the side of Russell that was loyal to his friends, but he was less fond of being treated second class.

"I started to drift off," he said.

Russell's sleepy smile was more open than the guarded mask he'd worn for dinner. "Careful."

Skip laughed. "Fifteen minutes' shut-eye, and I'll be good as new."

"I could drive."

Russell looked just as tired as Skip felt. "Let's find a room." The odds for finding a motel at this time of night weren't good, but Skip didn't want to sleep on the highway either. "There's a place about a quarter mile back with its vacancy sign lit up."

"Did it look decent?"

Making a show of it, Skip scanned the parking lot and surrounding street. "I didn't see any ax murderers when we drove by."

Russell scraped his fingers over the top of his head. "Good, because I've had enough drama for one night."

"Amen to that." Skip turned the engine on and put the car in gear, hoping they were both too tired for anything more than sleep. Skip didn't regret fooling around with Russell, but he sure as hell wished he hadn't offered him a place to stay. It was like he'd given the guy a knife and told him exactly how to cut out his heart.

The night clerk at the Lee Motel offered them separate rooms, but Skip protested, arguing they could save two dollars by sharing.

"The bed's a double, but I can bring you a cot," the clerk said. His shirt was clean and pressed but the hotel logo on the pocket was frayed around the edges. Pretty much like the rest of the place, Skip guessed.

The motel boasted air-conditioning, but the night air was cool enough they simply opened a window to clear the stuffiness. The cot took up most of the free floor space. Russell slipped the chain lock into place on the door, pulled the drapes shut, and Skip found he didn't have anything to say.

Russell took his turn in the john, then crawled over top of the cot to get to the bed. He lay on top of the covers, shirtless, his broad shoulders bronzed by the sun.

Skip had to tear himself away from the view.

Working quickly, he sluiced his face and armpits with water that smelled like oil. He didn't have a toothbrush, but he rinsed his mouth. He'd have rinsed other, more private places, but he didn't have the right tools for that either. Nerves twitched and fluttered in his gut like moths around a bare bulb.

It had been so long since he'd spent the night in the same room as a man, he didn't really know where to start. And with the way Russell blew hot and cold, he didn't really know if he should.

The cot creaked as Skip wrestled the thing into a comfortable position. The double bed didn't look like much, especially with Russell taking up most the space, but he bet it didn't have a metal bar running up the middle.

He found a position that didn't hurt and shut his eyes. They'd left the bedside lamp on. The room was silent except for the purr of cars on the highway and Russell's heavy breathing. Between the bar and the lamp, though, no way was Skip getting any sleep.

From the cot, he couldn't see Russell's face, but a shift in the mattress had him crack his eyes.

Russell was staring at him.

"Turn off the light," Skip said.

"What are you doing?"

Skip curled on his side, arm bent at the elbow to support his head. "I'd thought about sleeping some, but the light…"

Russell splayed his hands out on the sheet. "I thought you were just messing up the cot in case anyone came in."

Skip almost laughed at the puzzled expression on Russell's face. He wriggled around, twisting the top sheet between his legs, promising himself he wouldn't weaken.

Russell shifted over to his hands and knees, facing him. "Get up here."

Skip sat slowly. Russell had been blowing hot

and cold since they'd met, and if this was just one more flip-flop, he wasn't interested.

"You don't have to sleep down there."

Skip got his feet on the floor and his fists on the bed. "You sure?"

Russell patted the sheet, eyes dark, cropped hair rumpled.

Sure he'd live to regret it, Skip crawled onto the bed. He kept moving till he straddled Russell's thighs. Russell shut off the bedside lamp. Squealing brakes outside made them both jump, bringing them even closer.

"I just meant we could both sleep up here." Russell ran his hands up Skip's sides, strong and possessive.

"Just sleep?" Skip grinned, hearing the lie for what it was. Neither of them was being honest. He could imagine Russell telling himself he was just being neighborly.

A good neighbor who likes having his dick sucked.

Russell rocked his hips hard enough to silence Skip's reservations. In retaliation, Skip nipped him on the chin. "You're a monkey on my back, big guy. I can't say no." He thrust his hips once, twice, gripping the other man's waist to grind their cocks together, internal thermostat rapidly approaching the red line.

"Don't say no," Russell whispered.

"Shut up." Skip sealed his mouth with a bruising kiss, using physical force to drive off the fear of what the morning would bring.

# Chapter 16

&

"**D**OESN'T MEAN I'M NOT STILL frosted." Skip tossed Russell the car keys and climbed in the passenger side. He wasn't mad, exactly, just embarrassed to have given in and afraid of what he might have given away.

"Next time, you can sleep on the cot."

Skip gave him a squint-eyed glare. "Your good looks will get you in trouble one day."

Russell just smiled and put the car in gear.

Mom expected him to be on time for visiting hours, and they had a ways to go. "We're going to need to agitate the gravel to get there by two." Skip had a stop in mind before they got to Firland.

"I'll drive as fast as John Law will let me." Russell pulled the car onto Highway 99. They'd gone several miles, time Skip spent running through solo licks in his head, when Russell spoke up.

"How long has your mother been in the sanatorium?"

"It'll be a year next month."

"That's rough."

Skip tried not to talk about her illness, so he

didn't follow Russell's comment with one of his own. It had been rough, and there was no use in belaboring the point.

"Our neighbor was in the sanatorium for about four years," Russell said, his conversational tone inviting a response.

Someone with manners might have asked what happened. Skip didn't want to know. The neighbor lived or he didn't. Either way, he lost four years out of his life.

Years Skip's mother would never have another shot at.

They kept quiet all the way through Tacoma and the forest and farmlands of Federal Way. When they hit the city, Skip directed Russell to head back up onto First Hill. It was twenty minutes after one.

Russell cocked his head in a wordless question when they drove past the Sorrento.

"Need to stop at my apartment," Skip said.

"Did you forget something?"

"Not really."

In another block, Russell pulled the car to a stop in front of Skip's building.

"I'll be right back." Skip blew Russell a kiss, which made the other man squirm. "And bring you a treat for being such a good boy."

"Wait."

Skip paused, frowning when Russell climbed out of the car.

"I can just wait here," Russell said. "You don't want me hanging around."

But that was exactly what he did want, even though it made no sense. "Please." Seeing Russell would brighten his mother's day, and if she over-estimated things, he'd set her straight later. "Mom doesn't get many visitors. I'll make it worth your while."

He left Russell frowning on the sidewalk, and came back with a big box of maple bars and chocolate éclairs.

He handed one of the éclairs to Russell, who made a face. "You are the devil incarnate."

"Later I'll show you how I can suck out the cream."

"Hardy har har."

Skip settled into the passenger seat. "We've only got half an hour to get to Firland, and I hate like anything to be late. Let's get this chariot rolling."

They skinned in without an extra second. Russell parked in the lot in front of one of two gray-painted barns housing the sanatorium. The grounds were bare of plant life, and the whole place looked more utilitarian than healing.

"Used to be a Naval Hospital." Skip pointed Russell toward the main door, the box of maple bars tucked under his arm.

"You sure you don't want me to wait in the car?" Russell sounded nervous, but Skip was determined to introduce his mother to the first guy in forever to rattle his chain.

"Nah, come on. You'll like Mom."

Skip was careful to keep a cushion of space between him and Russell, because he didn't want him to go ape over something as stupid as a hand on his arm. He led the way to the main desk, a gunmetal contraption at the back of the bare front lobby. The young nurse watching the desk hadn't yet learned the frozen stare most of the others used on him. Her smile still had some heart.

"Hey Miss Jones," Skip said. "This is Russell. I've got some maple bars today. Help yourself."

Miss Jones blushed to the roots of her permanent-waved hair. "Hi, Lawrence. Hi, Russell." She took one of the donuts from the box. "Your mother's been moved back to the bed rest ward, Lawrence. I'm sorry. She's on the third floor."

Skip dropped his gaze to the floor. He had to swallow twice before he could get any words out. "Thanks, Miss Jones. We'll find our way there."

Disappointment and just plain sadness bogged down his spirits, filling his veins with sludge. They jogged up the stairs, Russell not quite touching him, a weirdly comforting presence. She must have had another hemorrhage. Skip's feet squeaked on the linoleum, and fear squashed his other emotions.

Skip stopped at the top of the stairs. "If we see a nurse, keep walking. Most of them act halfway between Napoleon and Attila the Hun, so unless they speak directly to us and demand we stop, just keep moving."

The way to the bed rest floor was painfully familiar. A nurses' station sat at the bend in the hall, and Skip stopped there reluctantly to ask for his mother's room number. Reluctant because he referred to the nurse on duty as Dracula's Daughter.

"I'm sorry, Mr. Johansen, but visiting hours are for family members only." Her nasal whine always ran about a quarter tone sharp. Drove him crazy.

"Russ *is* family. He's my cousin from Missouri,

and he's only here for another couple days."

Dracula's Daughter pursed her skinny lips and drew her cheeks in tight. Skip bit back a laugh. Who'd try to smuggle someone illegal into this hell house? Well, he was, but these were special circumstances.

"All right, then. Your mother is in room twenty-eight." She pronounced her verdict, and before she could draw a breath for a lecture, he headed down the hall. Russell followed, his footsteps soft in the gathering hush.

The place smelled like antiseptic, old blood, and pain. Skip had grown used to it, but a glance over his shoulder showed him Russell was trying to adjust. "Room twenty-eight is right down here."

Russell huffed a word Skip didn't catch. Might have been "Minnesota." Might have been "okay." Might have been "gonna barf."

Skip often wanted to barf in this place.

They reached the door to his mother's room. He gave it a quick tap and turned the handle.

"Skippy." Her raspy voice wasn't any louder than a whisper, the only sound left to a woman who used to sing torch songs with a band.

He crossed the room, doing his best to keep his face clear of what he felt. She looked awful. Worse than awful. She was pale, and she'd lost weight even since he'd seen her on Thursday. She lay flat on her back, a chartreuse dressing gown around her shoulders, her graying hair spread out over her pillow. "Hi, Mom. You got your hair done."

Her hand was as fragile as a baby bird in his grasp. "What's got that smile on your face?"

Most of the patient rooms had two beds running parallel along one whitewashed wall, across from a set of windows left open year round. The fresh air was supposed to promote a strong constitution, which the patients would need if they were to survive the cold. On this visit, the second bed was empty, so they had the room to themselves. Russell still stood in the doorway. "Come in," Skip said to him. "Come meet my mom."

Russell approached as slowly as if he were taking a long walk off a short dock, and for a second, Skip panicked. Bringing him here might have been a bad idea. Russell took a position across the bed and reached out his hand, the rigid lines in his face easing. "Hello, Mrs. Johansen. It's a pleasure to meet you."

So formal and correct. Skip gulped on the wave of emotions sluicing over his heart: pride and pleasure and pain. The warmth in Russell's tone nudged a few more points in his favor.

Mom touched his fingers, a light stroke, as if assuring herself he was real. "What nice manners you have." She took his hand more firmly, shot a glance at Skip. "He's a real gentleman, Skippy. And so handsome too."

"Mother." Skip couldn't stifle the heat rising in his cheeks. "He's standing right there."

Without letting go of their hands, his mother settled farther back in the bed. "You can call me May." Her smile was interrupted by a weak cough. "It's been ghastly, Skip." Her voice caught, and she started to cough again. She let go of his hand and drew out a napkin from a packet near her pillow.

He couldn't help but wince when she brought up blood with every spasm.

It took several minutes for her breathing to ease. When she was calm, she put the soiled tissue in a little bag hanging from her bed's rail.

"Did you bleed a lot this time?" he asked.

She scrunched her nose the way she had when he was a kid and she cooked cabbage. His grandmother claimed the vegetable was good for children, but they'd both hated the smell and the slimy texture. Mom served it every so often, though, because she wanted Skip to grow up big and strong.

Deciding she didn't intend to answer him, he changed topics. "I brought some donuts, and since you don't have a roommate, you'll have to eat them all yourself."

She smiled, an echo of the flirtatious young woman who worked in some of the most notorious nightclubs in the city. "You and your young man will have to help."

*Your young man.* Russell's eyes widened, but his smile never faltered, and Skip had another reason to be grateful no one else was in the room.

"Here, Mom. Let me get you one." Skip took a napkin and a maple bar from the box and set them on the table beside her bed. "Maple bar or éclair?"

"Éclair." She wheezed. "Tear it in half for me, will you?"

He broke the bar into three pieces. His mother picked the smallest, but at least she ate some. They chatted for a while about everything except her illness. She told him about the patient who'd been given a day pass to get married, and he told her about Long Beach. He made her promise she wouldn't give any maple bars to Dracula's Daughter, and she laughed and told him she'd save them for the night shift, where the nurses were younger and not yet so hard.

Too soon, a bell chimed. Time to leave. Skip squeezed his mother's baby-bird hand and bent down to kiss her forehead. "I'll be back Thursday, okay?"

"With more donuts, I hope."

"Good evening, Mrs. Johansen. I hope you rest easily tonight." Russell still held his mother's hand. She'd never let go of him.

"Thank you, Russell, but only if you call me May."

He smiled, tentative, a blush brightening his cheeks. "All right, May. You take care."

"I will." She squeezed his hand with enough force to turn her knuckles white. "And you take care of my son."

"I will."

They walked out of the building in a small clot of other visitors. Leaving his mother in such a depressing place flattened Skip's spirit. It usually took him a few hours to recover. This time, he had the additional worry about Russell. His mother's parting comment—to take care of her son—would have been fine if they were a couple engaged to be married, but put a lot of pressure on a man he'd known only a matter of days.

He couldn't decide whether saying something would make things worse or better.

❦

Later, at the apartment, Skip made good on his promise to demonstrate his technique with the éclairs, a process requiring candlelight and plenty of sucking. Russell liked the demo just fine.

Later still, shadows hung from the corners of the room like dusky velvet drapes. A single taper sat on the end table, casting a circle of gold around the bed. Russell lay flat on his belly on the bed, naked and exhausted, doing his best to suppress a grin. "You didn't need candles to seduce me."

"Sure I didn't." Skip straddled Russell's thighs like he belonged there, and Russell clamped down on his lower lip to keep from saying something foolish. He liked this man, though they only had a few more days. Talking about it would just make it harder to leave.

In response to the steady, warm pressure of Skip's hands on his back, Russell exhaled deep enough to quiet the chorus of insecurity still yammering in his head. They'd gone at it hard, even a little rough, a much better way to spend time than worrying whether Susie and Ryker would show.

Skip's knuckles dug deep into the knots between Russell's shoulder blades, making him wince. A groan started deep under Russell's breast bone, crawling out, carrying a load of leftover tension with it.

"I was just wondering…" Skip's fingers flexed across the steel belts running over Russell's shoulders as if he were playing a tune. "When did you know you were queer?"

The question bolted Russell's jaw shut. His first response, denial, shredded under the pressure of Skip's knuckles, the weight of his thighs, and the corresponding swell in Russell's own cock trapped between the bedding and his body.

Too honest to lie. Too scared to say anything at all.

When he didn't answer, Skip filled the silence with his own story. "I was about twelve or so," he said, "and one night, me and my buddies were looking for trouble down by Occidental Park."

He shifted, scooting farther up Russell's hips. Russell had to swallow another groan when Skip's cock—warm and half-erect—rested against his ass. Half listening, he basked in the strength of Skip's hands as the other man worked out the knots in his shoulders.

"Must have been nineteen forty-two or maybe forty-three," Skip continued, "and the whole place was full of grunts and squids, guys fresh out of boot camp and headed overseas." His strong fingers moved to the small of Russell's back.

Russell flinched, then exhaled into a sigh.

"A group of working ladies came past us." Skip's fingers fanned out along Russell's ribs. "Tight dresses and hair all curled. Lips painted red." He dug in with his fingertips and pulled back till his wrists met over Russell's tailbone. "My buddies stopped what they were doing just to watch them walk by."

With relaxation spreading through his limbs, Russell wondered at Skip's generosity, his open spirit. Russell wanted to repay him in kind, if he could find the courage.

"Then this GI came along. For some reason, he was in his dress whites, and the cut of his jacket made his shoulders look as huge as yours." Skip's fingertips traced a line along Russell's spine and across his shoulders, sending shivers in their wake.

His voice was soft, husky, seductive, and although Russell didn't want to dig into his own history, he found he couldn't move. He lay pinned by Skip's weight, his heat, and the growing regard he had for the other man.

"So that was it, you know? My buddies stood there arguing over who would get which working girl, and all I wanted was the sailor." Skip kissed the shivering skin between Russell's shoulder blades. "With Mom working down there, I knew a few queens. My wrist wasn't limp, but ever since then, I knew what I wanted." He smacked Russell's ass. "A broad-shouldered, clean-cut guy like you."

Quicker than thinking, Russell reached back and grabbed Skip's wrist, jerking him to the side. For a moment, they lay facing each other, breathing hard. Russell was taller, bulkier, and stronger. He'd also spent a lot more time on a wrestling mat in high school. With a quick move, he rolled over, pinning Skip to the bed. "You prefer clean-cut men?"

"Yep." Skip flexed his hips, pressing their cocks even harder together, and the intensity jerked the breath from Russell's lungs.

The rising moon added a silver glow to the candlelight around them. Russell tipped his head, unable to resist tasting the clean sweat from Skip's skin. He licked his way down the other man's neck, long and wet, rocking his hips slowly.

Skip twisted away. "Not till I've heard your story." His voice held a gasp, which fired Russell even more.

"Now come on." Skip tugged on Russell's hands, pulling them closer together. "My dick will argue if you try to tell me you're not a fruit."

The candle flickered, and Russell found a mark on the wall where an old leak took the shape of a spider's web. Talking scared him, fear annoyed him, but all his jagged emotions were muted by the delicate press of Skip's cock against his own.

"Why do you want to know?" Russell asked, delaying the inevitable.

Skip's laugh was warm and rich, distracting him almost as much as the smell of sex from the white cotton sheets. Russell gulped and tried to bring his attention in line. "I really don't remember much, anyway. Too long ago."

"Come on, Counselor. Don't hide the evidence." Skip ran his fingers along Russell's throat. "When did you know?"

"College." The memory could have killed his mood, but if anything, his cock hardened. That might have been Skip's fault. "My roommate was…older. He had a few friends…good friends… Fellows who could keep a secret." Between the group of them, Russell had experienced enough to know where his inclinations truly lay. "Everything happened behind locked doors." They'd acted like members of an informal club, where stroking each other off was the price of membership. "But then he and some of the others graduated, and I went home for the summer. As much as I enjoyed my time with them, I knew it couldn't last, so I started dating Susie."

There. He'd done it. He'd told someone else about his past. This small, dark room and these shared confidences recalled him to those days. Nothing that happened here would have any bearing on life outside, back in Red Wing or, God forbid, in his family home.

This door locked too.

"You killed it with Mom today." Skip squirmed, tugging Russell onto his side. Russell let himself be moved, relieved that Skip hadn't brought up any questions about his future girlfriend.

"It didn't even rattle your cage when she asked you to take care of me, and I...I owe you one." Skip paused, thoughts shifting behind his eyes. They lay quiet, belly to belly. "I keep telling myself to leave you alone, but I keep running right into your arms."

"And I keep catching you." In a different world, he'd never let go.

The silence was interrupted by a swell of chatter from outside. A group of people, all tenors and baritones, walked along the street under the apartment window. The burnt wax smell from the candle layered over the smell of sex, and an idea took shape in Russell's mind. As natural—as gloriously peaceful—as it felt to hold Skip, to feel the rub of his coarse hair against Russell's chest, he had to explain himself.

"Your mother is a lovely person," Russell began,

choosing his words carefully. Skip raised his chin as if he expected a blow. "My parents wouldn't understand us the way she seems to. They're...well, ever since Rory was killed, my mother doesn't smile." Russell wet his lips, as disappointed with himself as he knew his parents would be. Words alone wouldn't explain the shroud of sadness still wrapped around his family. "I thought if she had a wedding to get ready for, it'd cheer her up."

Skip's brow wrinkled. "So you were going to marry Susie to make your mother happy."

"No." Russell sagged onto his back, dragging Skip with him. "I was going to marry Susie because that's what a man does, but"—he shrugged, honesty forcing the words from him—"it would make my parents happy too."

Skip rose onto his hands and knees, crawling on top of Russell. "I can show you one or two other things a man can do to find happiness." His grin glowed through the semidarkness.

Russell ran his hand through Skip's hair, pulling the curls away from his face. "You've got till Wednesday."

# Chapter 17

**(**

PARKER'S ON A MONDAY NIGHT. There weren't many cars in the lot, but Skip had spent the whole drive over explaining how he'd talked the manager into giving them a shot. If Ryker and his drumsticks didn't show up, they might not get another chance.

Skip put his hand on the club's front door and blew out a deep breath, as close to nervous as Russell had ever seen him. "Knock, knock."

Russell reached over him to push the door open. "Who's there?"

"Anita."

"Anita who?" A couple approached, and Russell took a step to the side, holding the door for the woman.

With a lewd snicker, Skip grabbed his arm. "Anita dick in me." He spoke low, aimed right at Russell's ear, and his grin was full of the devil.

Suddenly sweating from far more than the late-August heat, Russell stumbled, trying hard not to laugh. His rational mind knew no one had heard Skip's outrageous joke. The irrational part of him was torn between embarrassment, lust, and a grudging admiration. Russell himself would never be able to joke about his perversion.

Maybe the laugh helped Skip shake off his nerves, because he moved like a thoroughbred, with confidence, grace, and control. After a day of playing house, Russell didn't see Skip's boxy jacket and slacks. He saw tight, toned biceps and the dimples at the small of his back. Following Skip across the room, he didn't see a slick, styled pompadour, he saw loose, sweat-drenched curls. He sidestepped a chair at the last second and swore he'd pay more attention to the scene around him and not carry on like some besotted schoolgirl.

The lounge was still mostly empty, the rows of round cafe tables covered in white linen lit by teardrop tapers. Two guys from Skip's combo were already on stage. Russell gave the room a cursory glance, but Ryker and Susie hadn't arrived. He chose a table to the right of the stage, near the front but not close enough to look desperate. A lone waiter dawdled at the long black bar, wrapping sets of silverware with snow-white napkins.

Customers filtered in. A man in a suit cornered Skip, who talked fast, acting much more confident than he had in the car. The other band members fiddled with their instruments, little snippets of melody rising above the crowd's chatter. Russell's nerves tightened with every stop and start. The band was supposed to go on at nine, but Ryker still wasn't there.

At three minutes till, Ryker and Susie walked in. Russell's heart slammed in his chest, and Skip watched his drummer cross the room with an unreadable expression.

Ryker wore black, his hair slicked in a greasy ducktail, his chin raised like he'd take the punch if Skip threw it. Russell cracked his knuckles, half tempted to throw one himself. Then he got a look at Susie's dress, a deep blue sleeveless number that showed off every one of her petite curves, and the fighting urge got stronger.

To distract himself, Russell looked around for a waiter. A shot of whiskey would calm him.

If it doesn't fuel my anger.

Susie surveyed the room with a movie star's air of boredom. The light haze of cigarette smoke shone in the stage lights, and some of the tables were still empty. She could have sat anywhere, but she strode over to Russell's table, a tiny princess in stiletto heels. After a pause, she brushed a kiss on his cheek and pulled up the chair next to him.

"I'm not getting on that train." She was made of sparkle and shine; her eyes glittered, her smiled glowed, and the huge diamond on her left hand played with the light like it was a pinball.

Russell plastered a smile over the dismay brought on by her statement.

Susie waved her petal-pink nails in Ryker's direction. "His mother's a Channing from Rhode Island." Her grin caught a calculating edge. "When Mom found out, the marriage was on, but she made us promise to wait till she could find us a church." For the first time all evening, she looked Russell full in the face. "So telling my mother won't do you any good. Mother talked to your Aunt Maude, and I'm skipping the Detroit shows because I'm getting married."

The waiter took their order, the band started a tune, and the empty tables filled with customers. Anything Russell said after Susie's announcement would come off as an argument, so he kept his mouth shut. He waved the waiter over and ordered them both a cocktail, giving them something innocuous to talk about. With a drink in his hand, he settled in to listen to the music.

Might have been a mistake. Skip owned the stage, his horn moving easily from plaintive sweetness to jubilation. He played raunchy too, his phrases sending shots of heat to Russell's groin.

"So Ryker tells me you're staying with Skip." Susie finally broke the silence.

Russell fought the telltale blush he could never control. "For now." Anyone who guessed what they'd been up to would cause trouble, but if Susie knew, he was done for.

"Does he have a house?"

*Shit.* "No, it's an apartment."

Susie toyed with her ring, twirling a spray of fractured light across the tablecloth. The heat and the clouds of cigarette smoke bore down on him. "Ryker says Skip's place is so tiny, you could fit it in a postage stamp. You must be sleeping in the bathtub."

Russell spread his fingers out over the linen table to keep himself from making a fist. *She knows.* Or she guessed. "I'll be leaving on Wednesday." As if the shortness of his stay could excuse his depravity.

As if Susie's forgiveness would excuse his shame.

Skip played the opening phrase of "Black Coffee," giving the tune more heat than Peggy Lee. Russell couldn't watch the band and couldn't think of anything to say, so he stared at his whiskey, humming along until the warmth of Susie's hand on his brought him to a stop.

"I hate Red Wing, Russ, and I'm never going to live there again." Her words were defiant, but there was an apology in her eyes. "I thought if I married you, we'd move to Chicago, or maybe even New York City."

"New York?" Flummoxed, Russell set down his glass. He had certainly never planned on such a big move.

"Well, I was wrong, I guess." She pulled her hand away.

Russell didn't know what to feel. He'd cared about Susie, sure, though if he were honest, Skip had him a lot more bothered. A glistening horn solo drew his attention. Skip reached him in a way Susie never had, even if he didn't want to give that feeling a name.

"Ryker and I get along, you know?" The prettiness of her porcelain skin left him cold. "His parents are going to buy us a house on the north end of the city."

Her prim little smirk almost tipped him over into anger, but then he had to laugh. He'd spent the last day in bed with another man. How could he stand in the way of her happiness? It didn't matter whether he wanted to be gracious. He had to be.

"Congratulations are in order, then." He raised his glass in toast. "I wish you all the very best."

She clinked her glass against his. "We used to be friends, Russ, before all this. Can we be friends again?"

Russell met her gaze. He would have given this woman everything. Then Skip laughed into the microphone, sending a shiver down Russell's spine. *Almost everything.* "I'd be happy to be your friend, Susie."

Skip grinned into the mouthpiece of his horn. Couldn't help himself. During his last solo lick, Russell's gaze had promised him something hot. Paddy's alto sax took the band through the chord changes one last time. Ryker got his big drum roll finish. Cymbals crashed. The song ended. The gig was done.

Time to pack the gear, pay the band, and go home with the best-looking guy in the bar.

Hard to keep the smile off his face.

"Man, I'm buzzin'. We've got to go out." Ryker hooted from behind his pile of disassembled drum parts.

Skip snapped his horn case shut, frustration dampening his excitement like fog rolling in off the Sound. Now would be a good time to scold Ryker for showing up late, but Skip didn't want to ruin his good mood. "Take your pretty girl home and blow off some steam."

Ryker slid his big crash cymbals into their black leather pouch. "I'll do that." He sounded down, as if he'd realized he might be in trouble. For a minute, Skip thought he might actually apologize.

"I'll see you at practice next week, then."

"Better be on time."

"Of course."

Ryker's indignation was almost comical. Skip stared out over the remains of the crowd so the drummer wouldn't see him smile. Russell caught his gaze, and one eye twitched. Either he had an allergy or he was a real subtle winker. The rising color in the big guy's cheeks matched the heat building in Skip's belly. Time to go home.

"See ya later, alligator." Skip hopped down off the stage. "I'm going to go find the manager so we can get paid."

Once they hit the car, exhaustion tried to drag him down. Skip had worked all day, and he'd been real keyed up for the gig. Russell's presence, though, acted as a tonic, and he couldn't wait to get the other man alone.

Walking into the building, he kept a fair distance between them. No use setting him off by accidentally bumping his shoulder. Excitement twisted his gut, shortened his breath, and numbed his fingers. They'd been working with their hands and mouths to find satisfaction, and it had been good.

Tonight, Skip wanted more. That knock-knock joke hadn't been all kidding. He needed Russell deep inside.

The apartment door closed with a soft click, then silence, as if the room itself was drawing a breath. They fell together, tumbling onto the bed. Skip rocked his head back, his hands roaming over dense muscle and warm skin. *So good*. He jammed his dick against Russell's thigh and dove in for a kiss.

He'd had been waiting all night for the taste of Russell's lips and the warmth of his tongue. Leftover excitement from the gig carbonated his blood, making him light-headed. Russell smelled of cedar, of growing things, of life, and Skip tore his shirt free of the waistband of his slacks. His needy hands stroked bare skin, though instead of relaxing, the sensation left him with more trouble breathing.

Russell licked along Skip's jaw, down to the tender place behind his ear, setting off flares of pleasure as he went. Skip thrust his hips, rubbing his dick against the other man's thigh.

"Take your clothes off," Russell said, his voice a husky whisper.

With the lights turned off and the blinds half-drawn, the room was too dark for Skip to read his expression. He reached down to unzip his fly, only to have Russell brush his hands away and take over the job. In return, Skip grabbed his shirt and dragged it over his head, then did the same with Russell's, making his strong, broad chest available to his hands and to his tongue.

When they were both nude except for Russell's boxers, Skip paused, one hand wrapped around the other man's dick through the thin cotton of his shorts. "I want you"—he gripped Russell's cock—"inside." He stroked, smearing moisture across the tip with his thumb hard enough so he'd feel the texture of the fabric. "Tonight."

Russell's dick pulsed, the only answer he seemed

willing to give.

Skip curled his fingers, stroked, leaned in, and tasted salty skin. "You won't hurt me."

Still no response. In his frustration, Skip clutched harder, gave his dick a yank, and bit down on the closest chunk of flesh.

"Hey now." Russell rolled to the side. "You don't have to go wild."

"But I want to." Skip wrapped his arms around the other man and pulled him so close, they could have been carved from one piece of stone.

The night air was humid, heated, sweaty. In the gray light, moisture gleamed on Russell's brow. His eyes were dark, his expression walled off.

"I like it," Skip said, trying real hard not to beg. "I like being held and having a man inside me."

Finally, Russell spoke. "I don't know if I can."

*Why not?* "Try."

Another pause. Russell's eyes closed. Skip's heart went into suspended animation.

"Okay."

Skip exhaled from somewhere south of his balls. "Okay." He cradled Russell's head in his hands and kissed him, gently, thoroughly, filling in the blanks, explaining how much he needed this.

He broke the kiss and gave Russell a little shove. "Strip. I'll be right back." He ducked into the bathroom and moments later returned with a silver foil tube and a smile. Russell leaned back on his elbows, his erection pressed against his belly. Skip stumbled, overcome by the perfect breadth of his shoulders, the feverish greed in his gaze. Before either of them could lose their nerve, he climbed on the bed.

"You've done this before." Russell muttered the words without adding a lift at the end to make it a question.

Skip let his smile grow, squirting clear gel into the palm of his hand. "Yeah, but not with someone I…"

Russell gave him a puzzled look, though again he didn't push Skip to finish.

Smearing the gel over Russell's dick, Skip hummed the opening lick of "I've Got the World on a String." The memory of the jam session when Russell sang made him smile. He could have done this then. Hell, he could have done it every night since. The man spread out underneath him touched a nerve, and not just the one pushing his dick into overdrive.

"This'll feel so good." Skip stroked and stroked, Russell's dick pulsing and jumping in response. "I promise it will."

Russell grabbed his wrist hard, fingers digging in and pulling, jaw tight. "That's the problem. I know you're right."

Skip was too far gone to give much thought to what Russell said. He squirted more gel on two fingers, reached around, and spread it over himself. "Please, Russ. I'll drive. You just lie back and enjoy the ride."

Taking hold of Russell's shaft, Skip positioned himself so he could slide the head back and forth across his opening. Russell gasped, biting down so hard, he turned his lower lip white. Skip preferred being underneath his lover, but for Russell's first time, he took charge. Cupping Russell's cheek with his free hand, he lowered himself.

They both groaned, relief hitting Skip so hard, he doubled over. Russell was thick, and the initial breach stung, so he gave himself a moment to relax before sliding down. Then up, thighs quivering. Down farther, the stretch and burn filling him. When he'd worked all of Russell in, the other man quivered, shuddered, gasped.

Still hunched over, Skip rose, taking things slow, still letting himself adjust. Russell lay propped on his elbows, head dropped back, mouth open. Leaning in, Skip licked his chin, traced a long salty line down his throat, and latched on to a nipple, licking and sucking till Russell gripped his thighs so hard, the nails cut into his flesh.

This was what he'd wanted, his big bull of a lover undone, the two of them forming a closed circle of need, sharing strength to create something whole. Russell's formal reserve shattered, and his lock-jawed grimace meant release was near. Skip picked up his pace and Russell matched it, his grunts rising in pitch, more whine than guttural groans, half-formed words. "Good. Good. This is good."

Hands sticky from the gel, Skip took hold of himself, stroking in rhythm. With every thrust, Russell hit his spot, intensifying the pressure. He wanted to get there right after Russell did, to give his lover pleasure before taking his own.

To share this central part of himself, the place the music came from, without the intercession of a horn.

"Ah Jesus," Russell gasped, his thrusts going from powerful to jet-propelled. He hollered, words too tangled to understand, and arched his back, fingers grinding into Skip's forearms. They hung suspended, one long moment of balance, then Russell slowly relaxed. Skip smiled, enjoying the random pulse of Russell's cock, the shuddering tremble working its way across his body.

Still stroking himself, Skip waited till the other man's eyes opened again before he spoke. "You okay?"

Russell stroked his cheek with so much tenderness, Skip had to blink away a burst of moisture.

"Sure. But if you ever say 'I told you so,' I'm going to cream you," Russell said.

Skip lurched, laughed, gave in to the sweetness. Russell wrapped both hands around Skip's dick, thumbs flexed to catch the tip with every stroke. Three pulls, four, and Skip let go, crying out his release and flying over the edge, shooting come across Russell's belly and chest.

He folded forward, rubbing himself on Russell, smearing warm come into his chest hair and skin. He jerked when Russell's softening prick slid out of his body, shivered at the brush of his lover's breath against his neck.

Once he had his breath back, he propped himself on his elbows.

"I know you'll be leaving soon," Skip said, measuring his words, trying hard to let his rational mind guide his emotions. He sure didn't want to care this much for a guy who'd be getting on a train. Care this much? *Hell*. How 'bout falling in love with him instead. "But if you ever—"

"I don't know if I want to leave."

Skip's heart dropped over a waterfall of emotion, then rose up, hopeful and happy. Russell spoke with deliberate defiance, and he wrapped a hand around the back of Skip's neck, tugging him down for a fierce kiss. "I mean, I know I can't stay, but I don't know if I can leave you either."

Heart going off like a piston, Skip didn't trust himself to speak. He rolled to the side, bringing Russell with him, scooting and tugging until the other man lay on top of him. Still no words would come. He pulled Russell in for a kiss full of wet, sticky heat.

It was the best he could do.

# Chapter 18

❧

RUSSELL FINISHED HIS CAN OF beer and stretched out on the bed. He'd bought a late copy of the newspaper from the rack out on the street. The small dining table was covered with want ads, and he'd even circled a few. He kept getting distracted, however, by the physical memory of Skip's body so warm and tight around his shaft, the dense velvet of Skip's ass under the palms of his hands.

He finally gave up trying to read the paper. He popped open a beer and settled in to wait for Skip to come home. They had some pretty big plans for Russell's last night in town.

Skip's Tuesday evening gig was a rarity, a midweek happy hour show, and he'd come close to canceling, but he needed the cash so he went straight from work. He expected to be back around eight. By nine, Russell began to worry.

At midnight, he called Harborview County and asked the operator if they had any new patients with Skip's name.

They hadn't.

By about three in the morning, anger and despair loosened their grasp enough for him to doze off.

Around eight in the morning, a delivery truck came to a stop outside the apartment building in a racket of squealing brakes and clunking gears, the perfect symphony for his mood. Still no word. He didn't have to be at the train station till noon, so Russell gathered himself, pocketed Skip's spare key, and went for a run. If he ran hard enough, maybe Skip would leach out of his pores in his sweat.

He traversed the neighborhood, past small shops and businesses somehow brave enough to open for the day. Childish, yes, but if Russell was falling apart, everyone else should be too. After about three miles, he stumbled over a stretch of wilderness. Good. A dirt trail disappeared through the trees, marked by a sign saying *Louisa Boren Park*. Dirt and brambles were a much closer match to his mood.

Russell hiked downhill through tall cedars, past shrubs covered with tiny, orange-pink berries. At the bottom of the hill, he took a seat on the trunk of a downed tree. His heart had slowed to near normal, and sweat poured down the sides of his face and between his shoulder blades. The bright sunshine they'd enjoyed since the Follies ended had been replaced by a high overcast and sodden humidity.

Physical exertion quieted Russell's most strident emotions, allowing him to look rejection straight in the face. Anything could have happened, but Russell's leading theory said the gig had given

Skip a chance to step back. He must have decided an uptight guy from the Minnesota wasn't worth the trouble.

Or maybe he'd run into one of his other boyfriends. They hadn't spelled things out, after all.

Or maybe he'd met someone new.

Or maybe...Russell gripped the tree trunk so hard, he tore off a chunk of bark. Chucking it into the bushes, he rose and began jogging along the trail. Uphill was a lot more work, but he was glad because it shut his damned head up. Skip would come back, and they would talk, and then he'd see what he'd see.

❦

The car door slammed, solid and heavy, and Ryker's Thunderbird rumbled away from the curb. Skip watched Ryker drive off, pretty sure he'd lost a friend. As bad as he'd wanted to lie, he'd told the truth, and Ryker would have to choose which parts to believe.

Skip would give Russell the same story, knowing full well Russell would be more skeptical. Ryker might suspect, but Russell would know, and because he knew the truth, he might not believe the cops had acted unfairly. The painful irony clawed its way through Skip's lineup of anger, fear and shame. What a mess.

But May Johansen hadn't raised a weakling. Skip squared his shoulders, tightened his grip on his horn, and squinted into the silvery glare of the high overcast. More than anything else, he wanted to curl up someplace quiet, some place he could rest. But he couldn't. Not yet. Not till he'd had a hard conversation with the first guy to raise his flag in recent memory.

*Goddamn that Officer Murphy.*

He made it into the building and up the stairs. The hall had grown twice as long, its worn carpet covered in patches of light and shadow from the overhead fluorescent bulbs. By the time he reached his own front door, he had to stop and lean against the wall.

Gripping his key so hard the metal jabbed him in the palm, he took a deep breath. Then another. He could do this. He just needed to explain why he'd stood Russell up on his last night in town and wish him well on his journey. Skip didn't need to get all flowery about it. Just say a few words and hang on to his temper.

Russell looked up when Skip came through the door, his expression as flat as the slate-colored sky. Skip's heart dropped, but before he could give in to second thoughts, he ripped the bandage off.

"I…" Skip tossed his horn in the lone comfortable chair. "I, ah, got arrested last night."

The shame could have choked him to death, and Russell's silence made it so much worse. Nothing moved except the look in Russell's eyes, an understanding that took Skip's shame and thickened it, made it even harder to swallow.

"What?" Russell's voice scratched out the word.

"Arrested." Pain exploded in his gut, and Skip bent over the chair, resting his forehead in his palms. "For lewd behavior." Though he really wanted to crawl away, he gulped a mouthful of air and forced himself to face Russell like a man. "Didn't make it in to work today, so I lost my job." He'd had hours in a jail cell to consider what that meant. He'd have to leave town. The thought made him sick.

Cars rolled up the street, black, red, white, some old, running rough and spewing dark exhaust, others new with shiny chrome fins. Russell's mouth seemed to be bound shut, but he sprang up, crossed the room, and put his hands on Skip's shoulders.

"Officer Murphy. He's"—Skip paused and cleared his throat—"he's been after me for months. Saw me parked over by the Greyhound station." He could have avoided the night in jail if he'd just given the cop a blow job, but his pride wouldn't let him. That knowledge fueled the nausea in his gut.

His own stupidity stung, and Russell squeezed his shoulders tight enough to make his eyes water.

"The bus station?"

"The club's down there. I just parked." Skip leaned away until Russell loosened his grasp. "I swear I just parked."

Russell took control, easing Skip over to the bed. He got them both sitting down, his arm around Skip's shoulders. There was kindness in his gesture, though his stunned silence hurt.

"So you called your boss?"

"Didn't need to. They already told me if I was late again, they'd mail me my last check." Skip folded over and covered his face with his hands. He was talking too much. He'd meant to just apologize to Russell and send him on his way. "Damn, Russell. What am I going to do now?"

He really hadn't meant to wail like a girl.

Russell jumped up and went to the window, raking his fingers through his hair. He stood there for a minute, leaving Skip stranded, then turned deliberately, as if he'd made a decision.

"Here." Russell reached into his wallet and pulled out a wad of bills. "Put it toward your rent. I owe you for driving me around all week."

Skip felt like he'd been kicked in the balls. "What? That's it? You think a few bills are going to help?" Rage filled the vacuum in his gut. Rage at a world that wasn't fair, directed at a man he couldn't afford to love. "I've been putting up with your nonsense all week. You think I'm only good enough to fuck when you're not mooning over Susie or worried about your precious reputation.

"Well, I tell you what. That hurts." Skip's words came out in a fury, boiling over because he couldn't yell at Murphy, who'd finally made good on his threats. "And you know what else? I've been playing pretty regular, but once summer ends, the gigs'll slow down." Blaming Russell might be irrational, but he didn't care. "Without my job, I'll have to go down to San Francisco, where I can make some real dough."

"What about your Mom?" Russell backed away, fists clenched like he wanted to hit something.

"Stop." Skip shuddered once, hard. Russell had no right to see him fall apart. He could take that big body and all his hang-ups and go back to the Midwest where he belonged. Skip clutched the fabric of his grubby gig pants. "We had fun, but you and me are going in different directions now."

Skip stood and grabbed his horn, desperate to

get somewhere he could be alone. "Lock up when you leave. I gotta go…" His voice trailed off. He had no idea where he was headed. Someplace on a city bus, since his car was still impounded. Someplace far away from Russell, who was leaving anyway.

Someplace he could find peace.

# Chapter 19

## ❦

THE SLAM OF THE APARTMENT door broke Russell out of his stupor. He ran, flung it open, but Skip had disappeared.

The apartment had been quiet before, but now the silence weighed on Russell's ears. He stood in the doorway for a moment, doing little more than breathing, and came to a realization.

He, Russell Wayne Haunreiter, was an ass, a frightened little boy. In the few days they'd known each other, Skip had been nothing but kind and generous and caring.

And Russell had met his distress with confusion.

Skip deserved better.

His moment of insight brought him to a second conclusion, one that sat him down hard on the closest chair. He couldn't get on the train. Aunt Maude would never understand, and neither would his parents, but a real man stood up for his friends. Skip already meant more to him than almost anyone else in his life. He couldn't live with himself if he ran out now.

If Skip were a woman, Russell would know what to do. He'd find a job and find a house and take care of him. It might not work the same way between two men, but God help him, he was willing to give it a try.

With those ideas in mind, he showered and dressed and headed for the train station. He intended to cash in Susie's ticket and change the date on his own. Skip had to come home at some point, and he wouldn't leave for California without seeing his mother one last time. Russell just needed a couple of extra days to make sure his lover was okay.

On his way out the door, he pocketed the tiny diamond he'd bought for Susie. He still had twenty dollars of his own, and Susie's ticket should bring him another thirty. After the train station, he'd find a Western Union office to wire Aunt Maude and tell her he'd be late. Then he'd go looking for a pawn shop.

Near sunset, Russell caught a cab down to Pioneer Square. The cabbie teased him about slumming on Skid Road. Russell did his best not to say something rude. Short-tempered to the point of being mean, Russell had his hands full already. He didn't need someone waving a red flag like he was some kind of bull in a ring.

The cab left him in front of the totem pole. The air was still muggy and hot, and Russell wore a pair of slacks and a suitcoat, so by the time he jogged down to the tavern, he was sweating.

The expression on Demetrio's face when he

saw Russell made him sweat harder.

"Excuse me," Russell said, doing his best to act contrite. He extended his hand, though he didn't really expect the doorman to shake it. "How are you tonight?"

Demetrio scowled, his brows a solid black line above his eyes. "What do you want?"

"Skip." Russell pulled his hand back, beyond worrying about something so trivial. "I'm looking for Skip Johansen."

Demetrio crossed his arms, resting them atop his big belly, and laughed. "Look, I don't know what you did this time, but Skippy don't want to see you ever again."

Russell scratched at the back of his neck where the barber had trimmed too close. "You know he got arrested, right?" Russell dropped his hands, gut churning. "I handled things, um, badly." If explaining things to a doorman on the street made him into an even bigger idiot, then so be it. "I'm going to hire a lawyer. I want to help."

Demetrio gave him the kind of look that peers around inside and takes stock of everything in there. "You serious?"

"Yes."

"Second to the last booth. Guy's name is Jack Dodson. He's a lawyer, and a good one." Demetrio nodded, black eyes still calculating Russell's merits and demerits. "Hire him, and I'll talk to Lou."

Russell said thanks, surprised and grateful to have found a lawyer who might understand.

He found an older man sitting alone at a booth in the back of the bar. Jack Dodson was slender, with a receding hairline and a just-get-to-the-point gaze. Russell introduced himself and dropped Demetrio's name. Jack invited him to sit down.

Russell slipped out of his jacket and hung it on a peg at the end of the booth. "Thank you for talking to me, Mr. Dodson." He slid behind the table. "I'm hoping to engage you on behalf of a friend of mine."

Jack flagged the bartender. "Order a drink, and we'll talk."

Russell waited till he had his first sip of whiskey. Then he talked. "My friend got arrested for lewd conduct, and I want you to defend him."

"How?" The man stirred his own drink with a skinny plastic straw. "It'll be his word against the cop's, and he'll lose."

A good lawyer could always find a loophole. "Anyone around here tried to change the precedent like Dale Jennings did in California?" Almost despite himself, Russell had made a study of the man who'd admitted in court to being a homosexual but denied he'd done anything wrong. A jury acquitted him.

Jack just laughed. "No, son, and I wouldn't take on your friend as a test case. The cops are easy enough to manage if you're willing to pay them off, but if a fellow did contest his arrest, he's likely to end up in the funny farm."

Russell fought against the tension in his shoulders, fueled by a rising sense of frustration. He'd always told himself his desires were perverted, but what he'd shared with Skip hadn't felt criminal, and neither of them was crazy. From Senator Mc-

Carthy on down, the government, the legal system, and all of society were stacked against them. "So what happens when Skip pleads guilty?"

"Likely just a fine. Sometimes they throw 'em in jail." Jack sipped his drink. "Who's your friend, if you don't mind my asking?"

"Skip, I mean, Lawrence Johansen."

"Damn." Jack's head snapped back, and he frowned. "I bet Murphy was the cop."

Russell set his glass down. "I think that's what he said." He scraped a fingernail along the lacquered tabletop. "I figure a lawyer can convince the judge to lower the fine or keep him out of jail. He already lost his job."

Jack's smile wasn't at all happy. "I can try." He tossed down some more of his drink. "Ten dollars up front, then forty more when the case is done."

Russell pulled out his wallet and put two twenties on the table. "Thank you. I'll have to mail you the rest."

"Wait a minute," Jack said. "What's your story? I mean, I've known Lawrence Johansen since he was missing his two front teeth and we all called him Skippy. Why are you helping him out?"

*Because I'm in love with him.* The words rang true, even though the shock of thinking them sent flames burning up his face. He took a solid pull off his whiskey, hoping the lawyer wouldn't notice his discomfort, and began to talk. He told Jack Dodson about the Aqua Follies, about Susie and Ryker, about graduating from law school and his thoughts about Seattle. Through it all, he talked about Skip, doing his best to describe how a charming smile and an open spirit had disarmed him so completely.

"So it sounds like you're thinking about staying here." The lawyer summarized Russell's story with a conclusion he had only begun to entertain.

"I would, but my parents need me back home."

"That's important. I always dreamed of bringing my son on as a clerk after he finished his degree so he could learn my practice for a year or so before I made him my junior partner." Jack took another sip of his cocktail, staring into some memory on the other side of the room.

His sadness infected Russell. "Didn't he want to be a lawyer?"

"He did." Jack's smile was bleak. "But he left school to join the navy and never made it home from Kwajalein." He shook himself and tossed off the rest of his drink. "Long time ago now. May's a strong lady, and the best thing she ever did for Skippy was buy him that horn. It'd break her heart if he left."

Russell inhaled deep enough for the whiskey to warm his belly, relief allowing him to relax some. "I don't want him to leave either. I just need to find him and tell him he's got a chance."

"Good."

Russell gulped the rest of his whiskey and slid to the end of the booth.

"Tell Skip to come by my office." Jack pushed a white business card in Russell's direction.

"Thank you. I will." Russell pocketed the card and shook the man's hand. He slid through the crowd at the bar, avoiding the gazes trying to catch his attention, and approached Demetrio. The bar's front door guy was talking to a pair of sailors who were looking for hookers. He acknowledged Russell with a head tilt and, after some jovial conversation, sent the sailors deeper into the Square.

"Did you work something out with Jack?" Demetrio asked.

Russell took out the lawyer's card, wishing he'd asked for another one. "Give Skip this and tell him to go see Mr. Dodson, please."

Demetrio took the card and tucked it into the front pocket of Russell's shirt. "He'll know how to find him."

Another quick handshake and Russell was on his way. He hiked back out to the totem pole in search of a cab, wondering if he should find a hotel. Reaching into his pants pocket, he fiddled with Skip's key. Skip had just said to lock up when he left, and Russell really didn't have the money for a hotel. He flipped the key between his fingers. If he stayed at the apartment, he'd be there if Skip came home.

❦

"Pass me the reefer." Skip kicked lazily at the coffee table in the center of the room. He lay sprawled across the couch, shirtless to cope with the late-evening heat hangover. The room was too small for all the ratty furniture Lou owned, and almost all of it was draped with floral fabric or covered with knickknacks. Staying with Lou was like visiting the grandmother Skip had never met.

The phone rang. From his spot sitting cross-legged on the floor, Lou mock-glared at Skip. "Answer it."

"Aw, baby, it's your phone." Skip let his head loll back against the bony ridge at the top of the couch. "You answer it." He grinned, pretty sure Lou wouldn't refuse him. "And hand me the reefer on your way by."

Lou made a disgusted noise and rocked onto his hands and knees, then struggled to his feet. He still wore the dress shirt required by his job at Bartell's Drugstore, but it flopped open, revealing the tight T-shirt underneath. The trim muscles across his chest flexed and rippled, stronger than would be expected for a man who often wore a dress. The familiar curve of his cheek and his wide, soft mouth tripped an old habit, an old desire in Skip, which threw him into a red-hot rage.

Because the idea of kissing any man, even one as familiar as Lou, brought him straight back to Russell.

And reminders of Russell hurt so bad, his heart, his mind, his soul shut down.

He stuck out his hand. "Gimme."

Lou handed him a marijuana cigarette on his way to the kitchen. The phone rang again, and Skip struck a match, inhaling deep enough to trigger a cough. He fought it, doubled over, forcing the smoke to stay in his lungs, to deaden his brain. He only smoked marijuana when he couldn't drum up any hope and needed to stop his mind from thinking.

The last time he'd done this was the day he left his mother at the sanatorium. This time he did it to deaden the shame.

He took another, more moderate hit, using the rush to ignore Lou's end of the terse conversation. Skip had his eyes shut when the phone handle rattled back onto its base.

"Who's calling here at this time of night?" Skip didn't really care, but Lou came over and stood in front of him, lips pursed like he had something important to say.

"It was Demetrio."

"Demetrio? What'd the old fairy want?"

"Russell went by the tavern tonight."

Skip scratched his belly, stoned enough to hear the name without losing his mind. "I'm hungry. You got any food in this place?"

Lou crossed his arms and thrust out a hip. "You know the answer, Skippy. Now listen. This is important."

"Do you still have that box of Ritz crackers?"

"I don't know." His tone was sharp with exasperation.

Skip shoved himself off the couch, a broken spring scratching at his thigh, and brushed past Lou on his way to the kitchen. "I think they're in the cupboard."

"Lawrence." Real anger replaced irritation.

"What?" Skip leaned through the door, a red Ritz box in his hand. "I'm going to get some butter to go with these." He ducked into the kitchen. If he kept his mind on the search for butter, he wouldn't wonder why Russell had gone to the tavern and why Demetrio had felt compelled to call them.

Lou still stood in the middle of the living room

when Skip carried out a bowl of Ritz crackers and the butter dish. He set the food on the table and rounded on Lou. "So are you just going to stand there and sulk?"

His friend's pretty mouth twisted, and he glared at Skip. "Stop being a dope."

"What?" he asked through a mouthful of crackers and butter.

"Your boyfriend went by the tavern tonight and told Demetrio he wanted to find you a lawyer."

Skip carefully picked up the knife and made a project out of buttering another cracker. "So?"

"He hired Jack Dodson. You're supposed to call his office tomorrow."

Surprise loosened Skip's hold, and the knife clattered against the glass butter dish. "It's a waste of money." He propped himself with his fists on the table. "Won't do any good. The cops live to throw fairies in jail."

Lou raised his palms. "Maybe. Maybe not. I hear Dodson does good work."

Skip dropped his head, hunching over the table. "Doesn't matter." He looked up, the bleakness of his situation ruining the mellow mood from the drugs. "No way I'm getting out of this without jail or a big fine."

With a heavy sigh, Lou crossed the room, putting his hands on Skip's shoulders. "You don't know that."

"I do." Skip arched back into the other man's touch. "I don't have a choice. At least if I'm down in San Francisco, I'll be able to earn some real chips with my horn."

Lou ran his hands over Skip's bare belly. "You can't leave, Lawrence."

"Got to, Lou. I already lost my job." Skip covered Lou's hands with his own. "The musician's union hears about this, and I'll probably get the boot." He twisted around so he could press a kiss to Lou's forehead. "I can't even teach kiddie lessons. What mother's going to leave a child with a convicted pervert?"

"Now stop it." Lou knocked his forehead against Skip's back. "Call Jack Dodson tomorrow, before you make a decision. You can always stay here, or maybe we can get a place together."

Lou would never leave his grandmotherly heaven, but arguing with him wasn't worth the fight. "Sure." Skip slid out of Lou's grasp and reached for another cracker. "Gimme the reefer."

Might as well stay stoned. As soon as tomorrow's visiting hours ended, he was on the road for San Francisco.

# Chapter 20

G

THURSDAY MORNING, RUSSELL SPENT HIS nervous energy on a long run. For most of it, the sky was the fragile blue of a robin's egg, and the sun was heating the air fast enough to make him glad he got his run in early.

Of course, once he'd showered and dressed, he had nothing to do. Nothing except sit in Skip's apartment, staring at the door, willing Skip to open it.

The telephone rang a few times, but Russell was unsure which party line ring was meant for Skip. He filled the time by copying the lawyers' names out of the phone book and composing letters of inquiry.

In a kitchen drawer, he found a city map and a bus schedule, and sat at the tiny table, trying to figure out how to get to the sanatorium. He couldn't get on the train without seeing Skip one more time. There were words he needed to say.

Gray shadows of defeat clogged his throat and made it hard to swallow. Visiting hours started at two p.m. Until the bus came, he had nothing to do but wait.

Midmorning, the room's ponderous quiet was disrupted by footsteps and a knock at the door. Russell rose quickly, hope rising even faster. *But Skip wouldn't knock.*

He hesitated. How would he explain his presence?

Another knock, louder and more insistent. "Russell Haunreiter, I know you're in there. Open the damned door."

"Susie?" She was the very last person he expected to see. He jerked the door open.

"I knew you'd be here." Susie's crisp white sundress all but glowed in the dim light, and her green eyes sparked. "Skip called Ryker with some kind of crazy story about getting arrested and said he'd run out on you."

"Yes, about that, um…"

She pulled off her gloves. A flat-brimmed straw hat sat at an angle on her dark curls. "And then he said something about leaving for California." She took off her hat and set it and the gloves on the table. Russell was glad he'd thought to put up the Murphy bed so he wouldn't be caught in an awkward situation.

"So I just figured we'd better stop him." She smiled like it was the easiest thing in the world.

Russell took a moment to organize his thinking. "I expect he'll want to see his mother before he goes."

"That's what he told Ryker, so we came to get you."

Her fresh, breezy confidence fairly took his

breath away. He was still trying to understand how she'd leapt so many steps ahead of him when she placed a gentle hand on his cheek. "Shut your mouth, Russ, you look like a fish."

Her giggle forced a smile out of him. "His mother's at a sanatorium, you know."

"Mm-hmm. Firland. Ryker's waiting for us in the car right now."

"But how did you know I'd be here?" The question burst out of him, and he was scared to hear the answer. At the club on Monday night, he'd had the sense Susie knew what Skip meant to him. He didn't know what he'd do if she guessed right. "Because you're a good guy, Russell Haunreiter. You wouldn't run out on a friend."

She patted his cheek once and dropped her hand, a shot of sadness dimming her glow for an instant. "Didja ever meet Uncle Bill?"

"Maybe once."

Her smile got soft, and she fiddled with her gloves. "He and his *friend* Edwin come over for Christmas dinner every year, but you know what?" She kept going without giving him a chance to answer. "My mother's the only one who'll invite them both. No one else in the family wants men like them around."

She looked him straight in the eye. "That night we went to hear the boys jam, back when we first got here, you and Skip were up at the piano. He said something, and you smiled at him, and I knew."

"Oh, Susie. I'm so sorry." She looked bright and brittle and proud, and Russell wanted nothing more than to wrap her in a hug. "I never meant…"

"I believe you." With a brisk shake of her head, she took his hand. "You would never have deliberately hurt me, Russell. I know that."

Neither of them had intended to hurt the other. She wanted a different life from the one Russell offered, and in the end, he wanted something other than what she could give. Russell let that knowledge sit, and for once, he spoke from the heart, without trying to persuade or argue or debate. "Thank you."

Her smile sparkled. "Let's go get your man."

Blushing, he pocketed his wallet and keys. Susie put on her hat and gloves and, laughing, led him to the car.

❧

In the lot in front of the sanatorium, Skip parked his car near a rhododendron that bloomed purple in the springtime, one of the only sources of color besides brown and green. This late in the year, the gray buildings stood stark and lonely. The rest of the city was weighed down with summer lushness, but not here.

Miss Jones sat in her usual spot behind the front desk, her hair a perfect helmet of curls, the swoops and angles of her lips making a promise Skip would never want to keep. He had to wait for the family of a new patient to check in before he could go through, hearing without listening to the lecture given to all families.

Miss Jones told them not to make noise.

She told them their patient must rest.

She told them even with the new, modern

medicines, their patient might die.

Skip forced himself not to hear the last part, instead staring at the harsh squares of sunlight on the glossy wood floor. He had to keep control of himself. He might be queer, but he wouldn't bawl like a baby, no matter what.

Finally, she waved him through. He would have jogged the whole way to his mother's room, but the nurses would scold, so he kept himself to a brisk walk. His mom was propped on pillows in bed, a porcelain doll with bisque skin and painted cheeks, so fragile a loud noise might shatter her. Her hair was pulled into a side ponytail and tied off with a ribbon trailing along her throat. He grasped her hand, gathering every ounce of nerve to get through the next few minutes.

"You need a haircut, Skippy," Mom whispered.

He brushed his bangs back from his face. "I've been busy."

In those three words, Skip telegraphed his distress. He hadn't meant to, had planned to be cool and calm, but his mother's brows drew together and she raised herself on her elbows. "What's wrong?"

"Mom, I..." Skip ran his palm over his forehead, picking and choosing from a dwindling supply of ideas. "I had some trouble."

"What?" She packed one word with worry and anger and fear, hitting him deep with the strength of her emotions.

He inhaled, exhaled, scrambling for the courage to say what needed to be said. "I got picked up by the cops...you know...and lost my job."

She nodded, showing him she did know. She'd

worked down in the square with the fruits and the addicts, with the colored people and the GIs, where everyone was just trying to make a buck to keep a roof over their head and some food in their belly. Skip wasn't an addict, so there was only one thing he could have been arrested for.

"Well, you'll have to find a new job." She sounded brittle, as if it took all her reserves to keep from giving in to panic.

Skip couldn't help her. "Not with that on my record."

She eased back against her pillows, lashes fluttering. She didn't cry any easier than he did, but she was close now. A child's laughter floated through the big open window, as if the universe itself thought there was a joke Skip couldn't see.

"I'm sorry, Mom." He pressed his lips together and stared at the ceiling until he could keep going without getting choked up. "I guess I'll go down to San Francisco."

She looked so stricken, he had to stop again.

"Jimmy Stevens has a band down there," he said when he had a handle on himself. "He wants me to be his first chair."

"No." A dry whisper, papery, like the pages of an old book blown by the breeze.

"I can make good money," Skip said, jamming some hope into his words even though he felt none. "I'll make enough to come visit every month. I promise."

"Oh, Skippy." Mom turned away, the small movement cutting him deep. "You can't leave me."

"I'm so sorry, Mom."

He had to leave. He was sorry. There was nothing else to say. He bent down and kissed her cheek, tasted the salt of her tears.

The very thought of her crying weakened his resolve. The evidence shattered him.

"No." Her voice firmed. "You're upset, and you should be, but you've got friends in this town, Lawrence, people who will help you out. You've got that young man…"

She was right, and he knew it. Lou would help, and Demetrio, and hell, Russell had hired him a damned lawyer. He straightened, rubbing his eyes with his hands so she wouldn't see him crying too.

"Don't be hasty, baby boy. Give it a month and see what happens before you take off." As if that proclamation stole all her energy, she faded into the bed.

Baby boy? She hadn't called him that in years. He bowed his head. A month would mean leaving in the middle of September. He'd still get down there in plenty of time to pick up holiday work. For just a second, he weighed the odds. Things would be slowing down here once summer ended, but they wouldn't be much busier in San Francisco, and here at least he knew people. The quiet side of him, the side he rarely listened to, asked whether he was leaving because of work or because he was ashamed to have been caught out for being queer.

*Good question.*

"All right. I'll give it a month, but if I can't make my rent, I'm really going to have to find work someplace else."

Instead of answering, his mother gave him an

exhausted smile. He stayed with her until she fell asleep.

Ten minutes later, he jogged down the front steps of the sanatorium. Someone leaned against the back of his Buick. His pace slowed. A broad-shouldered man, his navy crewneck tucked into khakis pressed in knife pleats down the front. Dark hair cut close to his scalp.

Chin tilted as if daring Skip to take a swing.

With a stern glare, Russell Haunreiter crossed his arms.

# Chapter 21

RUSSELL BIT HIS TONGUE TO keep from saying anything stupid. Skip came hurtling down the steps of the sanatorium faster than a football halfback. Or fast as a man would run if he'd just said good-bye to his mother and needed to leave before he chickened out.

Skip pulled up short, laughing. He ran a palm over his unshaven cheek. "What do you want?"

"To keep you from doing something dumb." Russell flared his shoulders, adding physical intimidation to the few verbal arguments he'd organized.

Skip shook his head with a wry smile. They mirrored each other, stances wide, chins jutting. The parking lot was empty of other visitors, set far enough from the main road to give them privacy.

Russell drew in a deep breath. He didn't have much to offer, but he had to try. "You don't need to leave, you know."

"You're right."

Russell barely heard him, ready to beg Skip to listen to what Jack Dodson had to say. "Because Ryker and Susie are going to buy a house with a basement, and they say you can live with them."

Skip squinted as if Russell was spouting nonsense. "Okay."

"And if Jack Dodson can get the charges dropped, you might not even owe a fine." The words tumbled out, and Russell could only hope Skip was hearing between the lines.

"Russell." Skip took a step toward him, his hand held out though they didn't touch. "I said okay. You're right. I'm not leaving."

Now it was Russell's turn to squint. "What?"

"I promised Mom I'd stay for at least another month." He crossed his arms, the growing assurance in his smile lightening Russell's heart.

"Another month," Russell echoed. The other man's capitulation left him flapping like an empty sail.

"I am surprised to see you, though." Skip came around to Russell's side and leaned against the Buick's rear bumper. "Thank you for retaining Mr. Dodson on my behalf."

Russell settled against the car, basking in the warmth of Skip's skin and the spicy smell of his pomade. "I couldn't leave without telling you…"

"Telling me what?"

Uncertainty nailed Russell hard. Could he really say this? "That I was…that I *am* in love with you."

Skip bowed his head and pressed a fist against his mouth. Russell took it as permission to continue.

"I may never say those words to anyone else." He scanned the parking lot for witnesses. No people, only the hot sun, the distant hum of traffic, and the endless blue sky. "And my train leaves tomorrow, but I'm coming back." He swallowed against the enormity of the emotion rising in him. "I don't want to live without you, and if I didn't tell you now, I'd spend the rest of my life regretting it."

Skip's bangs hung down so Russell couldn't see his face. They stood together in silence for long enough Russell began to plan for a graceful exit. Susie and Ryker had promised to block the driveway unless Russell was in the car with Skip. He took a step to the side, intending to ease away.

"Wait." Skip reached out and wrapped his hand around Russell's wrist, his dark eyes glossy. His expression made Russell's heart beat in double time. Hope expanded, warming and brightening Russell's soul.

"Coming back, huh?" Skip's voice sounded raw, as if it'd been pounded with stone.

"The shows in Detroit have already started. I promised Aunt Maude I'd be there, so I'll take the train tomorrow." Russell didn't even try to fight the grin. "After the run, I'll head home to pack my things."

"What time is it now?"

Russell glanced at his watch. "Two thirty."

Skip straightened his shoulders, his smile holding so much happiness, Russell had to look away. "Then we better get a move on." He loosened his grip on Russell's wrist, shifting his grasp to interlace their fingers, their gazes sharing more than the words they'd spoken.

"Let's go."

❦

"So what do you want to do on your last night in town?" Skip pocketed the keys to his Buick, the bulge in his pants giving his preference away.

Russell let his chuckle promise he shared the same interests. They still had things to talk about, but he wanted Skip alone and naked, and he was prepared to be as bossy as necessary.

At the apartment door, Russell turned, giving Skip his key back in a small ceremony, sealed—after a quick glance around—with a kiss that was more of a flash of lips against skin.

"You can do better than that, big guy." Skip jiggled the lock to the left, the quickest way to get the door open.

They stumbled into the apartment, Russell keeping as close to Skip as humanly possible. He shut the door, and the musician burst out laughing. "What?" Russell asked.

Skip stood in the center of the small room, arms extended, turning slowly. "I think this is the first time in about six months that bed's been put up."

Russell flopped down onto the upholstered chair and held his hands out. "C'mere."

Skip complied, landing hard on Russell's lap, legs swung over the arm of the chair. His warmth and lanky strength acted as a salve on the aching pain left by his absence, and in relief, Russell started babbling. "I didn't know it was possible to miss someone you just met. I didn't know…how good…" To stop himself from saying anything stupider, Russell pulled Skip in for a kiss, tangling their tongues, savoring his taste.

He didn't ever want to stop.

Skip smiled against his mouth, pulling away to rest his head against Russell's shoulder. "I know what you have in mind," he said, squeezing Russell's thigh, "but I need a shower first."

"No you don't." Russell's head dropped back as Skip nuzzled his neck, over the soft skin beneath his ear. Russell's cock was an iron bar in his slacks, and he could give a good goddamn whether Skip had showered or not. He stroked the bulge in Skip's groin, forestalling further argument.

Skip writhed against him, driving him even wilder.

"Jesus."

The need in Skip's voice spurred Russell to action. He went to work on the other man's fly, caressing his cock in the process.

"Shower." Skip might have wanted to say more, but Russell covered his lips with a rough kiss. Holding Skip's head in place so he'd shut up about the shower, he got both their flies open one-handed. He rubbed his thumb over the head of his own cock, then Skip's, using the leaking fluid to lubricate his grasp. Not enough. He broke the kiss, spit into the palm of his hand, and grabbed hold again.

Skip nipped along his jaw, nuzzling his whiskers. Russell stroked him, thrusting against his thigh. Skip groaned, and the vulnerability in the sound brought Russell right to the edge. Jerking frantically, he tried to hold on, but it was like trying to grapple with smoke.

Pleasure took him. He lost himself in the moment—the spicy-sweet smell of Skip's hair dressing, his strength and the softness of his lips, the overwhelming embarrassment for busting a nut so soon. And then he made it worse. "God but I love you." He ducked to hide his blush.

Skip was still hard, still thrusting, but lazy, gentle. "You keep saying the word, Russ."

His casual good humor made Russell smile through the awkwardness. "May never find someone to say it to again, so I might as well make it worthwhile." His heart was so warm, even that cold reality couldn't chill him.

Skip moved his hips in a slow circle. "Your jizz feels nice."

Russell snorted. "Can't help myself sometimes."

"'S all right. I really need a shower now."

Russell didn't need to look to know he had come smeared all over his belly, all over his shirt. They both did. Neither of them moved. Russell stroked Skip's shaft, long and slow in time with the needy grind of Skip's hips. The closeness, the heady scent of sex and smoke, and the afternoon heat combined to bring his own cock halfway back to attention, but now it was Skip's turn.

With only one night, he wanted to pleasure Skip, to worship his body, to prove his readiness to learn the lessons Skip had to teach. The other man had given Russell a glimpse of a different kind of life, and he wanted to repay him. He drove Skip to the edge and caught him when he went over. A part of him never wanted to leave.

They both dozed, there in the old chair, until the sticky dryness made Russell restless. With a soft laugh, Skip tilted his head. "So"—the word came out like a sigh—"if I write you letters, will you write me back?"

"Yes." Writing letters wasn't a perfect solution, but it would tide them over till he returned. "Yes, I will."

Skip cleared his throat. "I mean, or I could call you on the phone…"

Russell stopped, held his breath, gritty reality distracting him from fantasy. *What if Skip doesn't want me to come back?* "Do you want to?"

"Yeah." Skip's mouth worked as if he were afraid to smile. "You're not the only one who fell in love."

Russell stared, pure happiness welling up inside. "Really?"

"Yeah." Skip ran a thumb over his lower lip. "Guys like us, well, we don't find this feeling every day. I sure don't intend to let it go, to let you go."

For one brief moment, Russell let fantasy exceed reality. "Don't intend to let you go either." They might only have one more night, but he intended to make the most of it.

### ☙

Skip woke up early. Too early. There was a man in his bed whose grating snores broke through Skip's dreams. Russell. He'd be leaving at noon, and though he talked about coming back, Skip didn't really believe him

The morning sun landed on the roller blinds in squares of amber. The air was stuffy, already heating up. Skip couldn't move. He never brought men to his apartment, because he didn't want the traces

they'd leave behind, the echoes of Russell banging around in the shower and looking through the
cupboards for the coffeepot.

Dancing the cha-cha to a record Skip would
likely never listen to again.

Skip lay still, skin prickling where Russell's arm
lay across his chest. He couldn't weave together all
the patches of memory to fill a Russell-sized space.
They'd talked nonsense about what would happen
when Russell came back, and promised to write
letters every day, but what good would that do?

He'd brought the guy home, and now Russell
was leaving. Skip was pretty damned sure he'd never see him again. It already hurt.

Torn between getting up and huddling closer,
Skip wrestled with the thing that bothered him
the most. He understood the importance of family. He himself would likely be sleeping on Lou's
pink carpet to keep his mother happy. But Mom
understood him, knew who he was. Russell would
be going home to put on an act, possibly for the
rest of his life.

There was a difference between loyalty and
blindness. Fear could make it hard to tell which
was which. Skip rolled over, swung his feet to
the floor. Not fair to accuse Russell of cowardice
when his own recent lesson in caution still burned.
Maybe the guy had it right.

A strong arm caught Skip around the waist and
pulled him back in the bed. "Not yet." Sleep gave
Russell's voice a soft edge.

"I was just going to open a window."

With a move that would have taken down a

wrestling opponent, Russell flipped Skip into the center of the bed and pinned him. "Later." He dove in for a kiss, and Skip had no choice but to respond. And really, the rough scratch of morning whiskers and the burn of rising need were a satisfying way to put off heartache.

It waited, though, ready to wrap Skip in barbed wire and tear him apart.

# Chapter 22

❦

RUSSELL GOT ON THE TRAIN to Detroit with four dollars in his pocket and a belly full of grim determination. There'd be no replacement for Susie. He didn't want to leave home, but they needed lawyers in Seattle as much as they did in Minneapolis.

And Seattle had Skip.

Aunt Maude met him at the station. "I have some things to say to you, young man."

Biting back his first response—that the only thing he needed was a shot of whiskey and a warm shower—Russell found his aunt a smile. "I am sorry I was delayed."

She harrumphed, her perfect curls reflecting a sheen of disapproval. Over the course of the forty-hour train ride, Russell had drafted a letter to Jack Dodson, asking about a position. He'd also concocted a story to explain why he'd changed his tickets. It involved an imaginary hotel theft, and conveniently excused his missing diamond ring, in case anyone thought to ask.

He repeated the story so often over the remaining ten days of aqua shows that he almost came to believe it. At least until he got back to his parents' house and found a letter waiting.

The letter was signed, *Love, Skip*.

The team arrived home late Saturday night, and Russell spent Sunday morning in bed, writing his reply.

*Love, Russell.*

He was home, the land of tall trees, lakes, and ever-loving flatness. He surveyed his bedroom, the one he'd shared with his brother Rory, and crossed to the window to survey the street. All the same as he remembered. Then he dressed for Sunday dinner, because it was Sunday, and that was what he was supposed to do.

His mother had made a roast to celebrate his return, and the whole family would be there. By the time Russell came downstairs, the big cherry table in the dining room was set for nine. He couldn't avoid everyone, but he hoped he'd get through dinner without saying anything he'd regret.

"Good morning, sleeping beauty," his father called from the front room. "There might be some coffee on the back of the stove, but be careful or she'll put you to work in there."

Russell chuckled and kept walking. His mother would drop down dead before she'd let a man help in her kitchen. "Good morning, Mom."

"Good morning." His mother greeted him with a quick hug. Between the late-August sunshine and the heat of the stovetop, her cheeks had more color than normal. She wore a white apron over her drab Sunday dress, a string of pearls, and she'd twisted her hair in a perfect chignon. "How was your trip?"

"Fine." He helped himself to some coffee, stifling the riot of emotions. His trip hadn't been fine. It had been glorious and wonderful and devastating. He'd met the man of his dreams, and he could never tell a soul. The first twinges of a headache pinched his temples.

He set his letter for Skip in a low basket on the shelf near the back door. "Can I leave this here for the mailman?"

"Of course." His mother lifted a pot off the burner and set it in the sink. "Maude tells me you and Susie had a fight, so I didn't set a place for her today."

The headache settled in for the duration. "Susie stayed in Seattle. She's getting married."

His mother pulled a potato masher out of the drawer. "I'm sorry, dear." She dumped some butter in the pot and started mashing.

I'm sorry, dear? *Me too.* His mother's lukewarm response made all his worries seem foolish. Would she even care when he told them he intended to move? "I'm going to join Dad in the living room."

His mother hummed a response, her attention squarely on the dinner preparations. Russell took a seat on the couch and drank his coffee, subjected to his father's interrogation. He managed to keep from mentioning anything to do with Skip or Seattle, while at the same time his mind never left the letter. *Did I say too much? Not enough? Will Skip think I'm crazy if I write again tomorrow?*

The rest of the family arrived; his oldest brother

Robert and his wife, and his sisters Dumpling and Rayanne and their husbands. They each had kids, and Russell did his best to attach the right name to the right niece or nephew. He helped Rayanne set up a card table in the sun room for the kids to have their dinner, but beyond that, he mostly he kept quiet. He was tired of telling non-stories about his travels, and somehow, keeping Skip a secret only made him sadder.

He was so lost in himself he almost missed Dumpling's big announcement. She was the shortest of all of them, and three children had left her much stouter than back in her Aqua Follies days. After the family said grace, she raised her water glass.

"Mom, Dad, everybody?" Dumpling's round cheeks were flushed, and she gripped her husband's hand. "We have an announcement."

Rayanne squealed, Robert's wife started applauding, and Mom looked up from serving the roast beef.

"I'm having another baby."

Dumpling smiled so hard, it almost broke Russell's heart. A chorus of congratulations circled the table.

"That's nice dear," his mother said without much of a smile. "I hope you have a boy."

The conversation went on around him while Russell ate and drank until his head was pounding. Here he'd been so convinced a wedding would make his mother happy, and she'd been more worried about the potatoes.

Might as well get it over with. "I have an announcement too…"

They took it better than he'd expected. His brother and sisters were excited, and his father filled the air with bluster. His mother did little more than pat his hand, so lost in her own pain, she could barely respond. He finally made his excuses and went up to bed, but once he was alone, his thoughts still tormented him.

His twin bed sat parallel to the one his brother had slept in, until Rory had gone off to join the army and some Korean prevented him from coming home. What would Rory think, from his perch in the heavenly choir? Would he send Russell down with Beelzebub, or would he agree with Skip, that it was rare for men like them to find someone to love?

Didn't matter. Rory was dead, and Skip was halfway across the country. He might need to work for his father for a few weeks, to save up some money, but he'd made up his mind. Russell fell asleep with a belly full of roast beef and dogged determination.

ぐ

Skip swung the car door open. Ten o'clock on a Monday night. Time for bed. He tossed the horn case onto the passenger seat. A month ago, his alarm would have gone off at five a.m. Not anymore. He slammed the door shut and shoved the key in the ignition.

He needed consolation more than he needed sleep.

Fifteen minutes later, he parked his car on Western Avenue, a block away from Pioneer Square. The crowds were thick for a Monday night, so he'd find friends, people he knew, men who'd help cheer him up.

He crossed the ass end of Yesler to Second Avenue, stopping at the blind peanut seller's stand. The gnarled little man wore a greasy gray cap and had his shirt buttoned all the way to his chin, as if he could keep out the damp ocean air with frayed and dirty cotton. A pair of women came down Second, elbows and foreheads touching, skirts rubbing together as if they were trying to start a fire. They were clean and classy and obviously a couple, but after they crossed Yesler Way and passed the big totem pole, they drifted apart. They strolled along Second Avenue into downtown with a polite spread of inches between them.

Skip put a nickel in the peanut man's grubby palm and wandered along Second Avenue into Pioneer Square. Those ladies might snuggle in a Skid Row club, but outside they had to act like any other women—neighbors, coworkers, sisters. The same rules held for men, as much a part of his life as his horn and the smell of piss in the alleys. Skip didn't usually give it any thought. He popped a peanut and shook his head. Didn't seem fair. Maybe Russell was getting to him.

Demetrio greeted Skip at the door with a hug, which went a long way toward settling him down. "Your boyfriend is here, Lawrence."

Skip's heartbeat revved right up again. "Really? Russell's here?"

Demetrio patted his shoulder. "I meant the little one."

*Oh. Lou.* He chuckled at his heart's ability to generate hope so fast. "Thanks. I'll go find him."

"He's at the back of the bar, looking for trouble, if you ask me."

"Always is, D." Skip brushed past the clusters of men standing along the bar till he found Lou perched on the last barstool, wearing a white jersey and dungarees. His hair was parted and rolled and greased, and his lips were touched with light pink. Skip couldn't be sure if Lou'd dressed himself as a greaser or if Lulu was done up as a dyke.

"Hey, honey," Skip said, bussing Lou's cheek with a kiss. It had taken weeks for his friend to stop complaining about the smell of Mary Jane in his draperies, but they were okay now.

"Hey, yourself." Lou's smile was wide and warm. "Did you have fun at the gig?"

Skip flagged the bartender, giving the men standing nearby a surreptitious glance. "Not as much fun as you're having."

The bartender handed Skip a glass of beer. A wave of laughter crested over them, and one of the men at the bar stood up. He was tall and broad, like Russell. He wore his hair cut short and a dark suit, like Russell. He gave the man next to him a lewd wink, so full of promise it made Skip's blood burn, the way he dreamed Russell would.

"If you're looking at that bull at two o'clock," Lou said, his gaze traveling significantly in the same direction as Skip's. "He's mine." Lou pressed a knuckle into Skip's ribs. "Mine."

Skip brushed his bangs out of his face with a

sigh. "You can have him." The thought of talking to another man left him cold. If he got horny enough, he'd head over to the baths and find some guy to get him off. Dark and anonymous, where he could close his eyes and pretend he was with a certain swimming god.

"Your loss." Lou's grin was even sluttier than the man in the suit's had been.

Skip laughed and leaned against the bar. He and Lou made better friends than lovers because they both had the same taste. This one was too close to his sore spot. At some point, Skip would have to climb back on the horse with someone else. But not yet.

He was holding out, even though he simply couldn't make himself believe Russell meant what he said about coming back.

"Jack Dodson was here a little bit ago." Lou spoke without looking away from his target.

"Oh yeah?" Skip stifled the twinge of anxiety at the sound of his lawyer's name. "He's pretty sure he'll be able to talk the judge into giving me a fine."

Lou shot him a quick glance. "Better than jail."

"It would be if I had a hope of paying it."

Lou patted his arm. "We'll figure something out."

Kicking himself for distracting Lou from his manhunt, Skip changed the subject again. "Ryker asked me to be his best man."

Lou squealed and clapped his hands. "Are you going to do it? You look so grand in a suit."

"I said I would, yes." Despite his misgivings,

he'd agreed. It wasn't that he was jealous of Ryker's happiness. Far from it. He just wanted a little of that happiness for himself.

"And will lover boy be there?" Lou managed to target Skip's number one misgiving.

He snorted into his beer. "I can't imagine the bride's ex-boyfriend will want to drive across the country to see her marry someone else." Russell sent him a letter almost every day, and he signed most of them *see you soon*. So far, though, he hadn't set a date. Besides, in his last letter, Russell said he'd been offered a job.

That news pretty much shot down Skip's last hope.

## Chapter 23

&

THE CROWD ON THE DANCE floor swung in shifting circles to the rhythm of the big band, surrounded by a haze of cigarette smoke. Skip had first chair, which mean the back of his black tuxedo jacket was splattered with spit from the trombones. The band was rocking through the "Back Street Boogie," and for a little while, at least, Skip forgot to feel sorry for himself.

This Friday night dance was his one gig all weekend. They'd only just reached the first of October, and things were slowing down. Wouldn't pick back up again until the holidays. After that, it'd be a long, cold winter. When he visited his mother on Sunday, he'd have to break the news.

This time, Russell wouldn't be there to talk him out of a move south.

The band leader called for "In the Mood," a song that dragged him right back to Green Lake. Before he could fall too far into the well of sadness, he distracted himself with the monkey suit he'd wear for Ryker's wedding. Yeah, his new threads were unreal, and the party would be a gas.

Tonight was the bachelor party, and since Skip was the best man, Ryker had promised he and the other groomsmen would come by the dance. Flipping his chart between phrases, Skip gave the crowd a quick once-over to see if they'd shown.

They had. Susie and Ryker sat at one of the front tables, with the blonde Amazon Annette and a couple of Ryker's other friends. Behind them, tall and broad and gorgeous, stood Russell Haunreiter.

The sight squeezed the air right out of Skip's lungs, which made playing his horn a good trick. Light-headed, heart pounding, he tried like hell to keep his mind on the music. Getting through the rest of the set without embarrassing himself was something of a miracle.

Finally, the band leader called for a break. The musicians weren't supposed to fraternize, but Skip slipped off his black cutaway jacket and loosened his tie. Weaving through the dancers, the women in pastel dresses and pearls, the men in crisp slacks and sport coats, he kept his gaze trained on the table in the front.

Susie's black boat-neck top accented her pale skin and dark curls. Ryker looked smug, if a bit more wide-eyed than normal. And Russell? When he met Skip's gaze, the crowd's laughter, the clink of glassware, and the clouds of smoke all faded away, leaving only one smile in the room, maybe even in the whole world.

Skip shook Ryker's hand, kissed Susie's cheek, and grinned at Russell, hands in his pockets. Touching him was too great a temptation.

"Hi." Russell kept his hands in his pockets too.

"Welcome back." Just standing next to him spun Skip's crank, driving the specifics of polite conversation right out of his head. "There's girls at the bachelor party."

"You bet." Susie shoved her chair away from the table and stood. "C'mon, Annette. I need to powder my nose."

Annette made a little moue of protest and grudgingly climbed to her feet.

"And Ryker," Susie commanded, "be a doll and go get us some more drinks."

Ryker recruited his friends to help, leaving Skip and Russell standing by the table. "She's subtle," Russell murmured sarcastically.

Skip smothered a chuckle. "Listen…"

"When are you done?" Russell gazed out over the crowd, casual, like they did this all the time.

Skip brushed the hair back from his face. *Nothing to see here, folks.* "Ten, maybe ten thirty." The butterflies in his stomach threatened to send up an air raid.

"I'm staying over at the Burlingame Hotel on Olive Way. Room four-twenty-one." Russell spoke so quietly Skip was torn between leaning in to hear and stepping away to keep from dragging the other man down to the floor.

He kept his hands stuffed in his pockets, edging closer. "That's one of those residential places, isn't it?"

"I plan on being here awhile." Russell's smile broadened, but he kept his eyes on the dance floor.

Band members were filtering back on stage, and for the first time in his life, Skip really didn't want to play. "I guess you have a story to tell."

"Come by when you're done, and you'll see."

Skip's fists tightened till his knuckles cracked. No way could he say anything intelligent. He took a three steps toward the stage, turned, and held up four fingers, then two, then one. Russell's grin could have melted his horn, and Skip jogged off, laughing.

☙

The Burlingame was a wedge-shaped building that sat on a slice of land between Olive Way and Melrose, with a view looking out over downtown. Russell's room was small, barely bigger than the full-sized Murphy bed when he pulled it down from the wall, and the kitchenette boasted a sink, a small refrigerator, a hot plate, and not much else.

Compared with his room back home, it was perfect.

Russell pushed the dining table against the wall so there'd be space for the bed. He had two beers in the fridge but wasn't even sure they'd need them. In his bag, he had a stack of letters signed *Love, Skip*, so he wasn't worried his offer would get rejected.

Not *too* worried.

He left the blinds up, because no one could see into his third-floor room. Even if they could, the people on the street were mostly greasers and hipsters, and he didn't think they'd care.

Someone knocked at his door at about fifteen minutes after ten.

*Skip*.

Russell had to take a deep breath before he could respond, resting his head on the jamb, so excited, his teeth were chattering. A second soft knock brought him around, and he opened the door.

For a long moment, they just stared at each other. Skip had traded his tuxedo for a striped crewneck and a worn leather jacket, and his curly pompadour swooped higher than it had over the summer. His grin was the same, though, still full of charm and life and joy.

Without speaking, Russell took his hand and drew him inside, pausing only to lock the door before catching the edge of the leather and pulling Skip into his body.

Skip's hands flared out, finding purchase on Russell's shoulders. He licked his lips, then laughed, and Russell realized he'd mirrored the quick tongue flick.

"So…" Russell began a sentence, then got distracted by wrapping his hands around the musician's waist.

"So." Skip leaned against him. He smelled familiar, like pomade and cigarettes and sweat. They rocked their hips together, still delaying the moment when the barriers would fall and they'd kiss.

"Want something to drink?" Russell asked, forcing himself to be a good host.

Skip smiled. "Not really."

"How's your mother?"

"Better." Skip shook his head, as if he couldn't believe they were talking about something so mundane. "If she doesn't bleed any more, she may be home by Christmas."

"I need to get a record player so we can listen to music."

"Mine's packed away." Fingertips teasing the small hairs on the back of Russell's neck, Skip hummed a slow, sweet version of "Misty."

Russell's head tipped lower, almost outside of his control. "That'll do." *So close.* For the last six weeks, he'd spent every waking moment—and many of his dreams—wishing he had this man in his arms. Skip hummed, tipping his head, leaning closer.

Then they were kissing, a long, sweet meeting of lips and tongue. Russell all but lifted Skip off the ground in his eagerness to bring him closer. For his part, Skip scraped his nails through Russell's hair, his hummed tune turning into a heartfelt groan.

Long moments passed before they broke apart. "Come sit down." Russell drew the other man to the table by the window. There'd be time for the bed later. "I guess I should ask whether you're see-ing anyone else." He wanted to clear up his deepest fear right off.

"No." Skip settled into one of the straight-back chairs, still holding Russell's hand. "I told you men like us don't find someone to love all that often."

*There.* That word he'd waited six weeks to hear. "Didn't want you to get your hopes up." Russell shrugged, letting go of the tension he'd been car-rying since August. "I wanted to surprise you, you know? Jack, Mr. Dodson, I mean, offered me a po-sition, but I didn't want to say anything until I had his letter in hand."

"Well." Skip blinked, his smile softening. "I guess this means I can't move down to San Francisco."

"Not right away." Russell rocked their joined hands. "I want to tell you something else." He gulped, marshalling his arguments. "When I first came to Seattle, I really thought I knew what I wanted out of this life, but then I met you, and..."

Skip squeezed his hand, and, distracted, Russell brushed a kiss over his knuckles.

"I know the rules for dating women," Russell continued, "but now I want to learn how to go with men. How to be with you, because I love you."

"Russell."

"If you want me, I mean. I've done stupid things before, and I'll probably still make mistakes, and you'll have to smack me when I goof up." Russell blinked fast to keep the tears away. "You bring music to my soul, Lawrence Johansen." He gave in to temptation and slid out of the chair, landing on his knees. "Will you have me?"

Skip cupped Russell's cheeks, bending forward. "Yes." He whispered the word just before pressing a kiss to Russell's lips.

In a crashing wave of relief and happiness, Russell got his arms around Skip and pulled him down to the floor. Without breaking the kiss, he rolled so Skip was underneath him. "I hear the owner of this place turns a blind eye to overnight guests." He rutted against Skip's thigh. "So for now, at least, I figured we'd just play it by ear."

"Play it by ear," Skip echoed, chuckling as he

brought Russell's hand to his lips. "Good thing we can both carry a tune."

"Good thing you taught me to improvise." Russell dove in for another kiss, carried away with joy.

## *Acknowledgements*

THIS IS GOING TO BE a long one, because Aqua Follies has been such a journey. Just over three years ago, I saw a call for submissions for stories set in the 1950s. I had 15,000 words to work with, and a friend, Paula Becker, who's a historian. We were kicking story ideas around over coffee one morning, and she asked what I knew about the Aqua Follies, an annual production during Seattle's Seafair celebration in the 1950s.

To be honest, I knew nothing at all, but that soon changed. The other thing that changed was the romantic make-up of the story. I started writing about a young woman who came to Seattle to perform in the Aqua Follies. I thought she fell in love with a trumpet player in the band, but the words just did not want to come. Then I figured out that the person who fell in love with the trumpet player was the swimmer's coach.

The first incarnation went together easily and I sent it off....and got a lovely rejection. I sent the story to a couple other places, and got generally positive…rejections. Then I sent it to my agent, Margaret Bail from Fuse Literary, along with the following: I love these characters. Do you think the story would work as a longer piece?

Margaret was enthusiastic about Aqua Follies, so I decided to write the rest of the story. I'm old enough to just about remember the '50s…well, almost…and while stories set in that time period are definitely historic, it's possible to find first-person records describing what life was like. To supplement my research, I had a fantastic conversation with pianist Overton Berry, who knew from personal experience what it was like to be a jazz musician in Seattle in 1955. I also had help from the Musician's Association of Seattle, Local 76-493. Kirsten James and Monica Schley helped me find resources, and Paul Hanson helped with the make-up of a small orchestra and was even able to send me a pdf of an Aqua Follies program!

My friend Paula Becker came up with another timely assist, lending me her copy of The Plague and I by Betty MacDonald, an amazing first-person account of living in a sanitorium with tuberculosis. I could do a whole essay on Betty because she's something of a forgotten treasure. If my scenes in the sanitorium have the ring of truth, it's because of her and Paula.

When it was finished, Margaret sent it around to various publishers, where it got some favorable comments, but no offers. I still believed in Aqua

Follies, so I sent it to editor (and fantastic author) KJ Charles for a developmental edit. Her notes prompted a complete rewrite, which made the story even better. Along the way, I also got tons of feedback from my beta readers (and I hope I don't forget any…) Rhay, Amanda, Ellen, Debbie, Irene, Selena, and Ruth.

So, I ended up this great story that'd been tweaked and massaged and worked over many times. One of the recurrent themes we heard from publishers was that the mid-century time period was hard to place. I figured they didn't want to invest in something that might not sell. Given that, I decided to take the risk myself. I sent it to Linda Ingmanson for a final edit, connected with Kanaxa for the cover art, and voila…

Aqua Follies is here, and I do hope you enjoy it! And to the small army who propped me up during this process, thank you from the bottom of my heart.

I do want to give a special shout-out to my writing partner Irene Preston for holding my hand through the self-publishing process, and to my husband and kids for their unfailing patience and support. I'll turn off the laptop….in just a minute!

# Biography

**LIV RANCOURT** WRITES ROMANCE: M/F, m/m, and v/h, where the h is for human and the v is for vampire…or sometimes demon. She writes funny. She doesn't write angst. When not writing, Liv takes care of tiny premature babies or teenagers, depending on whether she's at work or at home. Her husband is a soul of patience, her dog is the cutest thing evah(!), and she's up to three ferrets.

*www.LivRancourt.com*

**Facebook** *www.facebook.com/Liv-Rancourt*
**Twitter** *@LivRancourt*

*Opposites attract, but secrets divide...*

RONNIE DURAND IS A COUNTRY boy who transfers to the University of Washington after two years at Central. He'll have to give up playing football, though finishing his education at a major university in Seattle—and being out and proud without having to look over his shoulder—makes the sacrifice worthwhile.But finding friends at a huge school is tough, especially when the hottest guy Ronnie meets makes him doubt his own sanity.

Sang's been on his own a long time. He's only a couple steps away from living on the street, and he's got dreams so big they don't leave space for a steady boyfriend.Then he meets Ronnie, who just might be strong enough to break through his barriers....as long as Sang lets him in on one big secret.

Made in the USA
San Bernardino, CA
04 June 2017